The
Adventures
of
Harry
Fruitgarden

Book #2
What's it All About?

By

Lawrence Vijay Girard

FruitgardenPublishing.Com

"Information and Inspiration for Living in Harmony with Life."

First Printing 2004

Chapter 1

The air was so hot that I felt like I was breathing through my sister's hair dryer. Once again I found myself in a long yellow school bus. This time I was sprawled on top of a huge pile of suitcases, backpacks and sleeping bags in the very back of the bus – it was the best seat in the house. As I looked up the aisle towards the front of the bus I could see thirty-nine more of my contemporary "city" boys. We were all headed to a summer camp in Colorado, but first we had to cross the Arizona desert with no air conditioning!

The last time I had been camping was with the Boy Scouts. We went to Crescent Lake in the San Bernardino Mountains outside of Los Angeles. That had been a lot of fun. It had awakened in me a desire to spend more time in nature. So when I heard about this camp from my Physical Education teacher at school, I ignored the fact that he wasn't high on my list of people to listen to carefully and opened myself up to the idea of spending two months in the San Juan Mountains of Southwestern Colorado.

Convincing my parents to let me go wasn't as hard as I thought it would be. When they heard that I wanted to go away for two months their eyes lit up. Hmmmm. Now that I think about it, maybe there is a hidden message there?

Well, I can be pretty prickly at times, but that's my charm! Or at least, that is what I keep telling myself. I don't actually seek to cause problems or get into trouble; it just seems to come my way. I attribute that to my creative approach to life. My grandmother just says that I'm stubborn. She might be right, but it seems like however I am, that is the way I'm made. You can say, "Tomaato" or you can say "Tomauto" but you can't say Harry Fruitgarden is boring!

My tendency to rub adults the wrong way has actually been a dilemma for me. You see some years ago, well…four to be exact, I had an experience that put some pressure on me to behave well. It wasn't something that came from my parents or anyone else. It was something that happened inside me - in my own self.

It isn't something weird like hearing strange voices in your head or anything. Maybe I should explain.

When I was eight years old I would sometimes find myself at my father's office. I can't remember my older sister ever being there, but I am sure my older brother and younger sister had the dubious honor of being in the real estate business for a few hours on Saturday afternoon.

Our main impression of the real estate business was that you sat at a desk and shuffled papers.

The exciting part was using the typewriter!

Back in those days there weren't any auto-correction buttons on the typewriters, not even liquid white correction fluid, to say nothing of word processors. If you made a mistake you had to use an eraser type pencil and rub out the offending letter. Most of our time in the real estate business was spent making more business for the correction pencil and the paper companies, as well as, the typewriter repair companies. As you can imagine, we would wear out our welcome at the office pretty quickly .

Fortunately for my Dad's office, as well as for us kids, across the street and up the block there was a miniature golf course.

I wonder if my Dad ever calculated the point at which it was cheaper to send us over to the miniature golf course than to repair his office equipment? Anyway, I think we thought our luck was pretty good. After all, how many kid's Dad's offices are across the street from a miniature golf course?

A miniature golf course is a kind of fantasyland where you can not only learn the futility of good putting, but explore the mind's realm of unseen possibilities.

As I listened to some of the golfers that I met while being on a real golf course with my Father, I had sometimes wondered if golf might be an inherently spiritual experience. I heard men pray for a good shot. I heard plenty of golfers ask God to "Damn it" or "Damn it to hell". I even heard an occasional "God bless it". Maybe they also had other requests for God that I don't know about. It even occurred to me that maybe golf was the same as religion since so many people went there on Sunday morning.

For me, it was miniature golf that lead to what might be described, not so much as a spiritual experience, but as a spiritual "situation".

My inner conversations with God started as the result of the very last hole on the miniature golf course. You know the one. It is the one that, if you get a hole-in-one, you get a free pass to play again.

After having visited the course a number of times I became a fair player for my age. I knew the object was to use the least number of strokes necessary to get around the course.

The more I played, I noticed that my focus began to shift from how I played each hole, to how I would perform at the last hole. I started to see the course as a kind of preparation time for the only really important putt of the whole course – that last shot for the free pass.

Once you have tasted the excitement of getting that hole-in-one and waving a free pass in the air as your victory flag, well…that is the Superbowl for a kid!

My desire for that experience welled up inside me to the point that I was desperate for victory.

I will never forget that day!

As I putted past the staggered blocks, over the little bridges, through the tunnel, over the bumps, down the slopes towards the windmill, my plight became more and more desperate. Oh how I wanted that hole-in-one at the end of the course!

How was I going to get it? What extra edge or hidden power could I bring to my side at this time of need?

And then it struck me.

God.

After all, if God couldn't do it, it couldn't be done. Yes, God was the answer.

While I putted around the corners and through the blocks, I began to think more seriously about how I could get God to intervene in this quickly approaching moment of need. Possibly because my father is a salesman or because I was brought up in a society that says nothing is free, or maybe all minds think that life is a bargaining table - whatever the reason - I decided that if I was going to ask God to do me this huge favor, I was going to have to offer something in return.

When I came to the windmill hole and started to mentally time the whirling blades as they passed the opening at the base of the wall, I realized that I didn't really have a whole lot to offer God.

What does God, Maker of the Universe, need?

And if God needed something that He couldn't get for Himself, how was I going to give it?

As I pondered the situation it came to me that it wasn't a question of God's need, but really of my desire. After all ... I was the one who wanted a hole-in-one. God was probably willing to let my ball roll where it may and not give it much thought.

I had to show God how important this was to me. I would need to offer something that wouldn't be easy to do. I reasoned that since Santa Claus' criteria for getting presents was whether or not a child was naughty or good, that might also be the gauge that God used. I would offer to be a good boy.

I really tussled with this for several holes.

What exactly was I committing myself to? Did God have specific requirements for what a good boy does or does not do? Did being a good boy include eating green vegetables at the dinner table? And, how long a time was I signing up for?

The seriousness of the situation was growing like a volcano. My mind and emotions were wrestling with the myriad of ramifications. That final hole was approaching with unwelcome speed. I still didn't grasp the whole of what I was getting into.

As I stepped up to that all-important last hole I felt that my eight years of life were suddenly on the line. I had somehow graduated from being a little boy playing miniature golf to a human being facing the most elemental of questions.

Does God really exist?

Can people talk to God?

Will He/She/It hear? And respond?

The moment was finally at hand. I hunched with concentration over that little round ball that now represented my relationship to the universe. With a sudden thrill of abandon my putter came to life and sent the little missile hurtling toward our common future. As it raced forward I inwardly gave the nod and knew that the deal had been sealed. God was now involved.

I no longer thought of what I had done. I watched that ball from a seemingly timeless perspective. The spinning ball appeared to move quickly and slowly at the same time. As it neared its goal I stood motionless. I was simultaneously intensely calm and wildly excited.

Suddenly I became aware that the moment had passed. My ears were the recipients of what seemed like a fanfare of trumpets. But it was really a very loud bell ringing to the world that the ultimate had been achieved. A hole-in-one!

I was delirious!

I raised my putter in victory. I grinned from ear to ear. I pranced to the counter for my medallion – a free pass for another round of miniature golf.

And as my little boy self rejoiced, there was my silent watchful self reminding me that I had made two commitments that day. The first was that I would try to be a good boy. I wasn't absolutely sure if God existed or not. As I thought about it I realized that I had struck a bargain with myself as much as with God. I knew I couldn't actually be good all of the time, but I did know that I had the choice of whether or not to try. By inwardly giving the nod I had committed myself to trying.

The second commitment was that a hidden well of interest in the spiritual nature of life had been awakened in me and I was determined that I would seek greater understanding about such things as opportunities presented themselves.

Yes, I was very lucky that my Dad had an office across the street from a miniature golf course. As I sat atop my throne of baggage in the back of the bus I inwardly smiled. Ahhh….that hole-in-one was sweet!

Just as I fully embraced the joy of that good memory a loud hacking sound came from a few rows in front of me. One of the boys was losing his lunch into a bag. The driver had warned us to keep bags handy for just such a need - apparently, he was an experienced driver. The sickly sweet odor wafted back towards me as the hot wind blowing in the windows came rushing through the bus. I quickly pinched my nose and looked the other way. I didn't want to join that unlucky fellow by losing my own lunch.

Whenever a boy wanted to know how much longer the trip would take, invariably someone would answer, " Ten more throw ups….or….fifteen more barf bags." Personally, I didn't even want to think about the subject, just thinking about it made my stomach feel queasy. I was pretty sure that folks would be more than a little upset if I heaved all over their stuff.

Here was a perfectly good question to which I didn't know the answer. If I threw up on people's baggage, would God consider that bad behavior? Certainly most of the kids would feel that I had done a bad thing. The driver would yell at me saying, "I told you to have a bag handy!" How was I supposed to know what is good or bad?

Mile after mile I wandered in my mind pondering these and other seemingly unknowable questions until the weight of my thoughts wore me out and I fell into a hot but restful slumber. Little did I know that even falling asleep would point me in the direction of trouble.

Chapter 2

"Harry Fruitgarden! Haaarrrrryyyyy Frrruitgarden! Where are you?" The sound of distant voices burst the bubble of my afternoon nap. Then the sound of big heavy boots came from the front of the bus and reverberated back to me where I had rolled off to the side of some backpacks to be hidden from view.

As I slowly emerged from a perfectly good dream about eating ice cream, the owner of the Paul Bunion shoes entered the bus and began to stride down the aisle towards me. I couldn't imagine what sort of trouble I could have caused while sleeping, but the since trouble seemed to be my middle name I was well used to people getting upset with me.

My vision started to clear just as Mr. Davis, the bus driver, approached me. He was a big man with curly brown hair. His ample belly jiggled over his belt and although he wasn't smiling, for a short moment he reminded me of Santa Claus. How I could have mistaken him for any length of time as a jolly old fellow struck me as a mystery. The only form of communication that I had ever heard from him seemed to be from the grouch school of thought.

As he neared me, in a flash I could imagine what he would say, "Well, you must be this Harry Fruitgarden that is always getting into trouble. Don't look so surprised, I know all about your escapades. I've been warned about you and I won't be putting up with any of your shenanigans. Now exactly what do you think you are doing in here?"

Here is another question that I have often pondered. Why do things seem to slow down when they get exciting? I've noticed this in many different types of situations. The more intense the experience the more time seems to get stretched. In a situation such as this, I felt I could think up a whole book of ideas between Mr. Davis opening his mouth and the sound of the words actually coming out.

Even in a sleepy daze I knew I could handle this type of situation. I would simply put on my puppy dog face and ask, "Excuse me, but what does shenanigans mean?" Of course I would have to keep a straight face - which wouldn't be easy. But I was experienced at such things. I could handle it.

Quick thinking didn't exactly prepare me for what Mr. Davis actually said. In a voice that was unexpectedly calm and friendly he inquired, "Are you okay?"

I was so surprised by the warmth in his voice that I just sort of sat there staring at him. He scrunched up his eyes and looked at me with concern. With a soothing tone in his voice he asked, "Are you sick?"

"No, I'm okay." I replied in a weak "What is going on here?" voice.

"Well, we were all outside looking at the Grand Canyon and someone realized that you weren't around. At first, Mr. Williams jokingly hoped that you had fallen over the edge. I didn't think that was such a nice thing to say. So when everyone looked around and didn't see you I decided to check the bus."

Grand Canyon? Everyone gone? I looked past Mr. Davis and my still slightly blurred vision took in the empty bus. I looked out the window but couldn't see much besides the lowering angle of the sun. I looked back at Mr. Davis and asked, "How long have we been here?"

"Oh, about 30 minutes." He replied.

It figures. Here we are at one of the seven wonders of the world and I am asleep in the back of the bus while everyone else is taking in all the wonder. Not only was I missing the Grand Canyon, but now everyone would tease me about not falling off the side of it.

I pulled myself together and said to Mr. Davis, "Thanks for coming to get me. I fell asleep and didn't even know we were here. Sorry I caused you to worry about me."

"That's okay." He responded. "I don't blame you for wanting to sleep during that long hot drive. I'd probably have done the same if I weren't driving. What do you say we go on out and have a look at the Canyon?"

"Sounds good to me," I said, as I pulled myself up out of the backpacks and scrambled out onto the floor of the bus.

As we walked towards the front of the bus I reflected on how my first impression of Mr. Davis wasn't the whole picture of who he was. At first I didn't think I liked him too much, but now I see that he has a pretty nice side to go with his grumpy side. It seems like I'll have to give more thought to understanding the whole picture of a person instead of just the side that is pointing at me when I meet them. Life certainly is full of things to think about.

As we stepped off the bus and negotiated around lots of cars and buses in the parking lot I began to take stock of my surroundings. The sky was a clear blue with just a few wispy clouds. The sun was low in the western sky, but still above the horizon. It was hot, but not as hot as it had been earlier. A weak breeze was moving the hot air, but not cooling it much. I could smell a mixture of desert and asphalt as we walked past a ranger station that had been blocking our view of the canyon.

I looked down and noticed some trash on the ground. Some birds were picking through scraps of paper and who knows what else? I stepped around them so as not to disturb their questionable meal. Then I stepped up a curb and finally my eyes rose to the view ahead and I stopped.

Stopping was followed by the dropping of my jaw and the widening of my eyes. My mind simply couldn't fully absorb what I was looking at. I slowly turned my head to the left and then even more slowly I turned it to the right. This was followed by moving it back to center where I continued to stare drop-jawed at the most amazing sight that I had ever seen.

When I had first seen the ocean I was impressed, but somehow I expected the ocean to be big. It is like looking up at the stars at night. The universe is all out there and it is huge, but it is supposed to be really big. When I heard about the Grand Canyon I expected it would be a nice valley in the desert, maybe a little bigger than your average valley, but this was waaaaaaay bigger. In fact I had to invent a new word to describe it. It was "biggerist". The most big: all the way to the moon big.

Mr. Davis had stopped next to me and was watching me as I absorbed the immensity of the Grand Canyon. I couldn't tear my eyes away from what I was looking at, but I did hear him chuckle and say, "Yea, it is big!" I knew that he knew what I was feeling and I appreciated that he didn't try to distract me from experiencing this first impression to the fullest.

It took me a full two or three minutes to compose myself and raise my jaw back up into its normal position on my face. I'm not sure if my eyes were bugging out or not, I know that they were fully wide open and I had no intention of letting them rest from drinking in this incredible sight.

Gradually I began to feel that I could step forward and explore my immediate surroundings. I was surprised to notice that there were a lot of people around. When I first looked up and saw the Grand Canyon I was so overwhelmed that it seems my ears withdrew from use so that I would have more energy to see with. Now I could hear everyone talking and see the others in our group milling around the low fenced edge of the Grand Canyon.

There were other tourists as well and I noticed kids of all ages from babies through teenagers. There were older folks that reminded me of my grandmother. There were couples that appeared to be my parent's age and then there were younger couples that seemed to cling to each other like they were afraid they might lose each other if they let go for a moment. Each small group seemed to have its own purpose and objectives.

The boys in our group were bunched together, pushing and jostling each other instead of spreading out to find their own spot. When they saw me they pointed at me and laughed. Normally I would have reacted to their taunting jokes, but in the presence of this canyon I couldn't be distracted by their empty words.

I didn't see Mr. Williams, which was just as well, I didn't want to get into an argument with him and waste a moment of the short time that I would be here. I knew just what I needed to do, but I would have to do it carefully so that no one noticed.

I turned to Mr. Davis. "Thanks for coming to get me Mr. Davis," I said sincerely. "It would have been a big loss if I had missed this."

As I looked straight into Mr. Davis's eyes, showing that I really meant what I was saying, he smiled and nodded that he understood. "Go on now," he said, pointing towards the Grand Canyon. "Get an eyeful while there is still enough light to see. We will be leaving shortly after dark to continue the trip, so don't wander off too far."

"Don't leave without me." I replied. "I have been too close to getting left behind before and it would be a mighty long walk from here."

"Okay," he said. "I'll keep my eye out for you."

"Thanks Mr. Davis." I said as I walked away, planning my next move while I stepped quickly toward the group.

Adults have often told me what a waste of time it is to watch television. I am sure some of the reasons that they say this are probably true. I have to admit that most of the shows I have seen are like cotton candy – sweet and sickening at the same time, and mostly just fluff. But right now I was about to test something that I had seen in a spy movie. If it worked then I could say that when I had been watching that show, I had been watching an "educational" show.

According to the spies in this movie, one of the best ways to disappear is in a crowd. I was about to test that theory in real life.

Ignoring the occasional jibe and poke from the other guys on the bus I slowly made my way through the middle of the group towards the railing. Squeezing my way in I kept moving forward. When I was just one boy from the railing I stopped, looked around, and listened.

I expected that the boys would be oohing and ahhing about the Grand Canyon, but they weren't. They were talking about sports, bikes and pimples. One of the boys farted and everyone broke out in laughter with lots of pushing, shoving and nose pinching. Then one of the boys remembered a time in school when someone farted in class and smelled up the whole room, but no one knew exactly who had done it. They all started to push and jostle each other again. Then they started to accuse each other of being the one who had done it.

I took this discussion to be my signal to push forward with my plan, or rather, to push over to the side. I made my way slowly to the left towards the edge of the group. Then as they seemed to erupt in new paroxysms of laughter and self-involvement, I quietly stepped away - thinking that those spy folks knew what they were talking about. Soon I had made my way around the curve of the canyon's edge, where it didn't take me long to put some distance between the group and myself.

Once I knew that I was in the clear I walked quickly. I was looking for what I call a special thinking spot. I would know it when I found it. My experience has been that when I need to sit alone and ponder life in general - and my life in particular - I can usually find just the right spot. It has to be private. Sometimes it has a view where I can look out and expand my thoughts, at other times it is more enclosed and I look more inwardly toward myself than outward toward nature. Here at the Grand Canyon I wanted to have grand thoughts that would reach out to greet the whole of this incredible place.

As I followed the winding edge of the canyon I eventually found a place where the path seemed to reach out closer toward the middle of the canyon. This was an outcropping that went slightly down hill and soon I was out of earshot of the group with no other tourists nearby.

At the end of the path I found a small break in the railing. I stepped through and sat down just on the canyon side of a bush - completely out of sight. I was not so close to the edge that it was dangerous, but if someone came up to the railing behind me they wouldn't see me.

Now I could let myself relax and fully absorb the glory of this magnificent place. My eyes wandered at will over the colors, textures, and shapes that made the canyon walls. Deep down at the bottom of the canyon I could see the Colorado River winding its way through areas that were green with trees and bushes. The hot wind carried the faintest wisp of the moisture below. The sun was setting and the last rays of the day were reflecting deep reds and browns on the far canyon walls.

A stillness came upon the land as often happens at sunset. I felt that stillness inside myself. My mind became calm and focused on the beauty that was before me. I found myself releasing all of the tensions of the trip and of my life in general.

I tried to imagine the endless number of years that it would take to carve out such an indescribably large amount of the earth. It was just so big that I couldn't fully grasp the immensity of Nature's task. I finally had to give up thinking about how it could be and just appreciate that it was. I gave myself up to the sheer wonder of it all.

After some time I noticed there was a big black bird soaring across the canyon;it fit so naturally into the environment. It didn't seem to matter what species it might be. It was big and beautiful, it represented all birds that soar. I envied that bird, being free to fly and explore the canyon from up above. Mentally I reached out to fly with it. Then, as had sometimes happened before, I felt released from the limitations of my body, I was no longer just a boy sitting on a hillside. My spirit soared out and embraced the beauty that was before it, I was no longer separate from nature. My body was still. My breath was still. My heart was full.

I couldn't say exactly how long I had been sitting there without moving. I had found a timeless space inside myself and I was reluctant to leave it. I heard voices approaching from behind and as they came closer I could hear some of the boys from our group griping again.

"Can you believe it?" One boy said. "Harry Fruitgarden is lost again. We couldn't find him when he was still in the bus, how are we going to find him out here at the Grand Canyon?"

"Leave him behind is what I say." Chimed in a different boy. Then the group moved off in another direction as sounds of general agreement floated through the air.

I was feeling so at peace that it took a few moments for the content of their words to make sense to me. They were saying that I was lost again, I didn't feel lost. Then I looked up and noticed that it was almost dark. Mr. Davis had told me that the bus was leaving just after dark. I had to get moving!

I jumped up, dusted off my pants and head back up the path. It took only a few minutes to make my way back to the bus. As I approached the bus I began to search my mind for a plausible explanation as to where I had been and why no one knew where I was. But before anything came to mind I found that the collar of my shirt began to pinch my neck and shoulder. The next thing I knew Mr. Williams was in my face while his right hand held a good portion of my shirt. He raised up his arm slightly and I went up on my toes to ease the stretch of my neck. He looked me right in the face and glared at me. He didn't say anything; he just gave me the evil eye.

As I sort of hung there wobbling on my toes, feeling surprisingly calm considering my current circumstances, I couldn't help thinking sarcastically, "Nice to see you too Mr. Williams." Of course, I didn't dare tell him that, but I did make one small mistake: I giggled.

Chapter 3

The thing about people who get angry before they think about what they can do with their anger is that whatever they do, it usually doesn't help them get rid of their anger. Mr. Williams was plenty steamed at me but what was he going to do? He couldn't hit me. He couldn't send me home. He couldn't even cuss at me - all of the boys in the bus would hear him. He could try yelling at me, but then what would he say? He didn't actually know that I had done anything wrong, he just hadn't known where I was. I wasn't even the last boy arriving back at the bus.

As I looked him calmly in the eyes I could see that the fire of his anger was burning hot. For some reason I felt detached from the moment and I inspected him like I would an interesting science project. After pondering the possibilities for a moment I decided to enter the experiment.

"Excuse me Mr. Williams," I said in my most polite but slightly choked voice. "I am having trouble breathing. Would you please release your hand from my shirt?

I could see Mr. Williams' anger flare for a moment; there was a sudden hush in the bus. Many of the

19

boys had their heads out the window as they watched with eager anticipation. When I saw he realized that there was an audience, I administered my final defense of his attack: I smiled.

He was dead in the water and he knew it. He lowered his arm and his eyes. As the heels of my feet lowered and met the ground I watched his face, but he wouldn't look right at me. After a moments pause he softly said, "Sorry. "

He tried to regain some dignity by telling me to get in the bus, but his voice rang hollow and everyone knew that he had lost our little battle. Unfortunately, I knew that he didn't consider the war over. As I passed him to get in the bus he poked me in the ribs with one of his fingers. He didn't do it really hard, just enough to let me know that he wasn't quite through with me.

As I came to the final step I looked up at the driver, Mr. Davis. He gave me a nod as I went by. Even though his expression was a little hard to read I had the impression that he was telling me something with it, but I wasn't exactly sure what the message might be.

The boys in the bus were quiet as I walked past them to my perch in the back of the bus. No one said anything, but I did get a few nods of respect from several of the boys. Most of the boys never needed to stand up to an adult - but they admired those who did.

I don't really like having to verbally joust with adults. I think that people of all ages should just get along because that is a nice way to live. But if they come after me with adult superiority instead of person to person communication, well, that riles me up a bit. When I get riled…well, I've been known to have a few adults backpedaling pretty quick after they tried to chop me down. Some people might think that I have a swelled head on this subject. I hope not. I'm not trying to be better than others, I just feel like there are times when a person needs to stand up for themself. And I just seem to run into more of those times than others.

As I climbed back up on the sleeping bags and backpacks I released my thoughts about conflicts and mentally played back the images of the Grand Canyon that had been etched in my mind. What an incredible place. I wish we were staying longer, I would have liked to climb down into the canyon and explore along the river. There must be endless great thinking spots in this place. I leaned back on my bed of luggage and let my imagination wander over the possibilities.

Now that it was night the air was cooling and riding in the bus was much more comfortable. After about an hour of driving Mr. Williams announced that we would be driving all night to avoid some of the daytime heat. We would be stopping at a gas station in about half an hour and anyone that needed to use the bathroom should do so when we stopped.

As we neared the gas station I started to think that I might need some late night sustenance. Some candy bars might come in handy later in the evening, so when we stopped I headed out to see what I could find. Mr. Williams stopped me at the door.

"Need to use the bathroom Fruitgarden?" Mr. Williams asked me.

"No, " I replied without thinking.

"Then get back to your seat." He said with a big grin.

"I just wanted to get some can…" I tried to say candy but Mr. Williams cut me off.

"Back to your seat." He pointed with his finger while expanding his grin even farther, causing his yellowing teeth to glow eerily in the glow of the lights that were on inside the bus.

21

It took me a moment to grasp what had just happened. When I thought about it I had to admit that I had stepped right into that one. I took it like a man and walked to the back of the bus with no comment. It appeared that little skirmishes were still to be won and lost, I would have to give some more thought to Mr. Williams.

As I was sitting in the back pondering what the summer was gong to be like with Mr. Williams as my enemy, Mr. Davis stopped by.

"How are you doing Harry?" Mr. Davis asked in a soft voice.

"Oh, I'm fine. " I replied. "I was just going for some candy, no big thing."

"Well, maybe I can help." Mr. Davis said. "What did you want?"

I gave Mr. Davis some money and told him to choose anything that looked good to him - which was probably a dangerous decision since I didn't know what his taste in candy was. But then I figured, what the heck, he was doing me a favor, make things as easy as possible.

After another twenty minutes everyone was back in the bus and Mr. Davis was back in the driver's seat. It looked like he wasn't going to be able to get the candy to me. As the bus pulled out of the gas station my stomach rumbled in harmony with the engine and I began to think that I would have to do something about getting that candy.

I was staring out the window watching the night sky reflect dim shadows on the desert landscape when a brilliant, yet possibly insane, idea came to me. In the spirit of the spy idea that I had used earlier I decided that I would use the redirection of Mr. Williams attention to allow Mr. Davis to give me the candy. Of course since

Mr. Davis didn't know of my plan, I would have to hope that he would catch on once I got things going.

Yes, this was going to be good!

I waited a few more minutes on the off chance that Mr. Williams would fall asleep. I didn't think he would so early, but I figured I could wait awhile just in case.

Mr. Williams was sitting on the right side of the bus in the first seat near the door. My plan was simplicity itself, all I had to do was put on my most sincere face and add some charm to my voice. Since the bus was in motion all of the inside lights were off. I hoped that the darkness would provide cover for Mr. Davis to give me the candy.

I made my way up to the front of the bus slowly; I was looking in the rear view mirror hoping to get Mr. Davis' attention without attracting Mr. Williams' attention. Since it was dark everywhere it didn't seem that there was much chance Mr. Davis would see me. When I was about six rows back from the front a big eighteen-wheel semi truck started to pass the bus on the left. His lights were bright and they flashed on the outside rearview mirror getting Mr. Davis' attention. Apparently the lights were too bright, so Mr. Davis looked to his right. Just then the reflection from the outside mirror flashed across the inside rearview mirror and Mr. Davis saw me in the aisle. I immediately raised my hand and opened and closed my fingers. He looked at me quizzically but didn't say anything. I just nodded back and smiled. It appeared that luck was with me. I pushed forward with my plan.

I stepped up to the front seat and turning my back on Mr. Davis as he drove the bus I faced Mr. Williams. Mr. Williams looked up at me in the dim light and after a moment he recognized me.

"What do you want, Fruitgarden?" He asked in an irritated voice.

"Well, Mr. Williams, I have been thinking about what happened earlier today and I just wanted you to know that it wasn't my intention to cause any problem." I said in my most sincere voice.

For a moment I thought I saw Mr. Williams face flicker with doubt, but then a smile appeared on his face. He seemed to feel that my apology was sincere: he was right and wrong. I wasn't lying about not wanting to cause trouble. I rarely try on purpose to cause trouble. But he was wrong about thinking I was apologizing: I wasn't. I was just stating the facts as I saw them. I never actually said, "I apologize." He just assumed that I was apologizing because he believed he was right and I was wrong.

As I had suspected he would, Mr. Williams began to wax eloquent about good behavior and the need to get along with authority. As he warmed up to his subject I slowly backed up toward Mr. Davis. As I moved back I placed my left hand behind me and stretched it back as well as I could while I opened and closed it - hoping that Mr. Davis would see the gesture and put the candy in my hand. With my right hand I scratched my chin while nodding my head up and down, causing Mr. Williams to do the same. When Mr. Williams hit his stride and started in on the need for youth to respect their elders, I began to wonder if Mr. Davis was going to catch on to my plan. Then I felt the candy touch my palm. I closed my grip around the candy and stepped forward reaching out with my right hand.

Seeing my right hand extended Mr. Williams understood that I wanted to shake hands on our new understanding. And since he apparently couldn't talk and shake hands at the same time, he stopped talking. I took the opportunity of our hand shaking to let him know that I was going to head back to my seat. He nodded that it was a good idea and I discreetly backed away so he couldn't see what was in my left hand.

It had worked flawlessly! The only thing that diminished my success is that I couldn't start laughing right then and there. Mr. Davis had really come through, I owed him one for that.

Back on my perch in the back of the bus I inspected the booty that had come to me with unexpected entertainment value. Now everyone was happy. Mr. Williams was happy, Mr. Davis was happy, and I was happy, one big happy...well maybe not a big happy family...but at least no one was mad any more. That was a good thing. I didn't really want to start the summer with Mr. Williams as my enemy.

As I munched approvingly on Mr. Davis' taste in candy I began to wonder what the rest of the summer would bring. What would Colorado be like? What would camp be like? What would I do all day? Would I make any friends? I heard they had horses at this camp, what would horseback riding be like?

I stared out the window and let the desert darkness and the cool nighttime air flow through my hair and my mind. I relaxed and soon I once again fell into a peaceful slumber. My last conscious thought was of horses, I think I was concerned about getting stepped on.

Chapter 4

I'm not sure if it was the sun, the rocking of the bus as it bounced along the highway, or simply some internal clock calling "Wake up now!" that roused me from my slumber. I became aware that it was daytime when I quickly covered my slowly opening eyes because of the all-too-bright sunshine that was coming in the windows on the eastern side of the bus.

Most of the other kids were still asleep, so the bus was relatively quiet except for the sound of tires and wind coming in through the windows. Once I got used to the sunshine I lay on my pile of baggage and looked out at the seemingly endless desert. On both sides of the road there were different kinds of cactus, stunted trees, and bushes that looked like they hadn't seen water in a long time. It was amazing to think that life could exist out here in the heat. I saw what I thought was a buzzard circling high in the sky. It occurred to me that it was probably looking for breakfast. I didn't really want to think about exactly what that might mean.

Gradually the other boys woke up and started chattering. Most of the talk I could hear was about what they thought their breakfast might and/or should be.

26

French toast and pancakes seemed to be on the top of most people's list - that sounded pretty good to me. A few boys wanted eggs and hash browns, while one poor fellow mentioned oatmeal and was booed heartily.

That got me to thinking about my all time favorite breakfast: matzo brei. - which is fried matzo. I am surprised that more people don't know about it. My grandmother taught me how to make it. Matzo - which is unleavened bread from the Jewish Tradition – is moistened with water and then mixed with an egg batter. The mixture is then fried like a big pancake – some people scramble it like scrambled eggs, but I prefer the pancake style. It is important to use lots of butter during cooking so the edges get real crispy. When it is done cooking you put more butter and then maple syrup on top. All I can say to truly communicate the experience is: Yummmmmmmm!

Just as I was about to take a bite of my mental picture of the perfect breakfast, Mr. Williams stood up and announced that we would be stopping soon to eat. While general cheers of enthusiasm went up from the hungry group, I tried to hold onto my inner vision of the sweet syrup as it mixed with melted butter and dripped off the sides of a big mouthful of the best …but I couldn't do it. The moment was past, my concentration was broken. So now I would have to reconcile myself to whatever breakfast was in store for the whole group.

When we stopped a few minutes later in the parking lot of a supermarket I didn't see how that was going to lead to breakfast. After about twenty minutes Mr. Williams came out of the store with a cart full of breakfast cereals, milk, paper bowls and spoons. Soon everyone was lined up to choose their favorite cereal. There were plenty of pre-sweetened choices like Trix (which I particularly like) and Frosted Flakes. There was also some

Shredded Wheat and Wheaties (which as far as I can tell is a glorified way of saying bran flakes). Actually, those kind of flakes really aren't that bad as long as you put plenty of sugar on them. If I don't have any sugar I sometimes mix pre-sweetened and un-sweetened cereals together. That seems to do the trick.

Breakfast went pretty well except for a few dropped bowls of cereal and one boy who almost choked on a mouthful of trix that he just tossed into his mouth dry. He must have gotten a few caught too far back in his throat before he could chew them. The next thing we all knew he was gasping and then spewing partially chewed Trix out into the air. A couple of guys had to leap out of the way quickly, but no real harm was done. Once it was clear that he was going to be okay everyone started laughing – including the boy that did the choking.

It was what happened after breakfast that turned our group into a real circus. We were 40 boys and two adults that had just spent the night traveling in a bus with no stops during the night. And now everyone had just filled up with breakfast. The cereal dealt with the bad breath well enough for everyone but the dentist. Since showers were out of the question there was some ripeness in the air, but guys can ignore that sort of thing as needed. But no one can ignore the need to go to the bathroom.

At first thought you might think, "No problem, there is a gas station next to the market. Just use their bathroom." But when that gas station has only one toilet in the men's room and there are forty guys that need to make room in the lower part of their bodies for the breakfast that has just entered the top…well, that could be a problem!

It took a few minutes for everyone to figure out that there was about to be a serious line in front of the bathroom. When I noticed the need myself I looked over to the gas station and saw ten guys waiting in line. Some of them were already moving around with that "I really gotta go" shuffle. Then I noticed that Mr. Williams and Mr. Davis were conferring, pointing at the line and looking around. I instantly realized that I needed to make a decision about what I was going to do. I took a quick survey of the small shopping center. There were only a few storefronts next to the market. It was too early for most businesses to be open. When I saw a Laundromat at the end of the shopping center I didn't hesitate for a moment.

I didn't want this to turn into an all out sprint by ten or twenty boys to see who could get there first, so I did my spy, shuffling thing, and worked my way slowly away from the group. Trying not to be noticed I just kind of backed up with the thought that not turning my back to the group would keep people from thinking: Where is he off too? Which might lead to them figuring out there would be a bathroom in the Laundromat. I actually made it half way across the parking lot before Mr. Williams and Mr. Davis noticed me, saw the Laundromat sign and made the connection. I saw grins come across their faces and I watched the wheels turn in their minds. We were all three eye to eye. They didn't want to advertise the situation either; they needed to go bad just like everyone else.

I was tempted to yell out to everyone and make a sprint for it. That way Mr. Williams would have to run or wait longer. But I decided that I couldn't do that to Mr. Davis, so I kept my mouth shut and turned to walk the last few feet to the door.

In the end my calling out to them wouldn't have affected things. As I pulled open the Laundromat door I heard a loud yelling sound behind me. I turned back to look and saw that a group of boys had figured out what was going on. All at once they started to scream and run towards the Laundromat. Mr. Williams and Mr. Davis had apparently not been practicing their invisible walking away technique. When Mr. Williams and Mr. Davis realized the secret was out they started to run as well. The whole thing was such a comical sight that I started to laugh. That delayed my forward progress until my mind caught up to the fact that I had better find the bathroom before they all arrived.

When I turned and looked into the Laundromat I saw a row of dryers on the left side of the room and a row of washers on the right side. I didn't see a bathroom. I was about to panic when I noticed that there was a space on the right wall at the end of the washers, in the very back. I ran past the washers and looked to the right; what a beautiful sight! There was a men's and a women's bathroom. I ran to the men's room and jumped in through the door. It was a single toilet, so I quickly shut the door and locked it.

No sooner had I gotten the door locked then I heard a loud clamoring outside followed by an even louder banging on the door. "Let us in!" someone was shouting. I didn't for a moment consider doing so. It wasn't that I didn't care about them. I could certainly sympathize with their need. I just, well, needed to go really bad and figured I may as well take care of business.

When I was done in the bathroom I was greeted in the hall by a flurry of "What took you so long?" and "Oh, My God, What a stench!" I didn't take any of it too seriously. I was just glad that I had been in the front of the line and not at the back. I didn't even want to imagine what it would be like at the end of the line.

As the bus started to fill back up with relieved fellow travelers there was a lot of laughter about the situation. The poor boys who had to wait the longest were still bravely doing what they could to deal with the situation. Some of the boys in the bus took sadistic pleasure in watching the waiting boys squirm. It was a testament to the human body's ability to endure adversity that none of the boys soiled themselves that morning.

Soon we were back on the road. The day was heating up quickly and the desert seemed to go on endlessly. One of the boys started the, *Ninety-Nine Bottles of Beer on the Wall*, song and soon the whole bus was going at it with vigor. While that isn't my favorite song, as I sat in the back of the bus and noticed that the swaying motion of the bus was rocking back and forth to the rhythm of the song, I felt compelled to join in. The group merged together and swelled with one multifaceted voice. We entered a kind of group harmony and all seemed well and good with the world. The youthful ardor didn't abate even though it took some time to work our way down through the numbers. Occasionally one of the boys would just whoop out with a loud expression of unbridled enthusiasm. Everything was beautifully on track for a successful completion of the song when at twenty-three bottles of beer on the wall one of the boys gave up their breakfast to one of the barf bags.

The boy was in the front of the bus so I hardly noticed that it had happened. When we got to twenty-one bottles of beer on the wall and another boy decided that breakfast had to go I did take notice. The group kept going and I kept singing, but concern was trying to raise its head up in the back of my mind. I decided that I should increase the loudness of my singing to distract myself from what was going on in the front of the bus.

When we got to nineteen bottles of beer on the wall and two more boys had let loose with their breakfasts I became very concerned and stopped singing. At eighteen bottles of beer on the wall the group faltered

31

seriously when three more boys lost their breakfasts. Then the most serious assault on my equilibrium arrived; I sniffed the odor of throw up in the air; that is never good. I felt the contents of my stomach stir and I realized that I had to take charge of the situation or I would be joining those boys who had woefully barfed before me.

The, *Ninety-Nine Bottles of Beer on the Wall,* song never made it to sixteen, because I yelled in my most full throated and expanded lung voice, "Stop the Bus!"

To my amazement the bus did actually pull off to the side of the road and stop. While it was slowing I stuck my head way out the window and took a full breath of odor free air. Then I forced myself back into the bus and started up the center aisle as fast as I could towards the front. I was careful not to breathe or look at anyone who might be in the act of throwing up. By the time I got to the front the bus had completely stopped and I looked past Mr. Williams at Mr. Davis.

"Open the door, I'm getting off," I said as I expelled my breath and determined not to take any new air in until I was off the bus.

When Mr. Davis looked at me and I bugged out my eyes and nodded my head towards the door he got the message. He opened the door and I jumped down the stairs and walked away from the bus taking deep breaths of fresh, non odorous air. Soon the bus was mostly empty, including the adults. Everyone spread out to be safe just in case their neighbor started to let loose with their breakfast.

After about half an hour Mr. Williams checked the bus for odors and then asked everyone if they felt okay to get going again. I was in no hurry to get back on the bus. I hadn't thrown up, but it had been mighty close. I wasn't sure the other boys were going to be able to keep things from starting up again. At the same time, I didn't see that we had any choice but to keep going.

I was the last one to step up onto the bus. As I passed Mr. Williams he called out my name, so I looked over to see what he wanted. It occurred to me that he might be mad at me for stopping the bus. He looked at me right in the eye and said, "Good call, Fruitgarden." And then he actually smiled.

Chapter 5

As the hours passed and the sun climbed high in the sky a quiet settled over the boys in the bus. The excitement and queasiness of the morning had worn everyone out. Most of the boys were trying to sleep, daydreaming or simply staring glassy-eyed out the window at the passing desert. Mr. Williams had taken over driving the bus and Mr. Davis was hunched over asleep where Mr. Williams had been sitting in the front row.

Somehow my wandering attention had found its way to a boy on the right side of the bus two rows up from my perch on the luggage. His name was Bob Welch and I knew him from school. We weren't close friends or anything, but we knew each other. He was pretty good in sports, so most of the guys at school liked him. Since I wasn't too good at sports, I had never spent much time with him.

Bob was surreptitiously picking his nose. He apparently thought no one was watching for he was going at it pretty vigorously. I suppose I should have averted my eyes from this private moment, but I was strangely fascinated. Or maybe I was just really bored. Anyway, I was watching him when he apparently got the feeling that someone was watching him and he whirled around to find me looking before I could turn away.

Now that was an awkward moment!

Bob just froze when he saw me watching. The index finger of his right hand was substantially hidden in his right nostril. Then as our eyes locked he slowly removed the finger - as if by locking his eyes to mine I wouldn't notice what he was doing. When his finger became fully visible, with a huge booger on the end of it, my gaze uncontrollably switched from his eyes to the tip of his finger. Seeing my eyes move their focus he turned his head to see what I could see on his finger.

As I took in the sight of Bob looking at his booger, I saw Bob's eyes go wide. I thought I could see embarrassment, shock, and a little bit of wonder flash through his face.

No sooner had he visually taken in the gooey mass then he twitched his finger as if he had found a dark hairy insect that was about to bite the tip of his finger. He shook his finger with such force that the booger was flung across the aisle towards a boy who had his eyes closed and appeared to be asleep. When the wet mass landed on the boy's right ear, the boy stirred slightly.

Removing the booger from his finger seemed to remove the distance between Bob and I. Now we were both watching something that was completely out of our control. We became co-conspirators in a secret that no one else in the world knew about. Both Bob and I watched to see what would happen.

We didn't know this boy who had inherited the booger. There was no malice intended toward him. An unexpected turn of events had presented itself and we were just watching to see what would happen.

The back of the bus was quite susceptible to the bumps and undulations from the road. So there was a constant shaking and jostling that took place as the bus made its way down the highway. This motion was causing the booger to sway and then to extend downwards. When the boy moved his head slightly - as if to shake off a fly - the booger moved even more and we had to stifle the urge to laugh.

Unfortunately for the booger's innocent victim that movement of the head caused the sticky glob to move further down the ear. As it moved, it apparently caused a stronger tickling sensation to reach the boy's brain, which caused him to raise his right hand towards his head. Bob and I were starting to lose control of ourselves and let some sounds of laughter escape our hand covered mouths. Just as the boy's hand was about to reach its target the boy's eyes opened and in that moment when his hand reached the offending sensation on his ear, he whirled around and saw me looking at him and laughing. Instantly I knew that once again unintended trouble was heading my way.

Maybe I should have yelled at him to stop his hand, but there wasn't really time for me to think. He wiped his palm against the side of his head and the slimy mass was spread all over his ear. As he pulled his hand away and inspected the sticky mess it didn't take long for anger to fill his eyes.

It must have been the endless hours in the bus that dulled my brain. It took me way too long to figure out that I was about to be under attack. The boy was half way to me before I realized that I was going to need to defend myself.

I had been lying with my head toward the front of the bus. The offended boy - who was bigger than me - came running toward me and literally dove up onto the baggage straight at me. Just as fate seemed to be against me in causing this problem, fate entered the picture again by causing a larger than average bump in the road just at the right time.

The boy was so mad that he had launched himself with substantial strength in order to get at me. Fortunately for me, the force of the bus moving in an upward direction just at that moment caused the boy to fly up higher and farther than he intended. So as he went up and over me, I slid forward and landed on the floor of the aisle in front of the baggage.

As the offended boy attempted to turn himself around and get back at me, I scrambled to my feet and looked back. To Bob's credit, he jumped up into the aisle between myself and my assailant. As the boy climbed down from the heap of baggage Bob tried to calm him.

"He didn't do it!" Bob yelled at the boy.

The boy kept coming and Bob used his hands to push the boy back.

"He didn't do anything!" Bob said again firmly. "Let me explain."

The boy's face was red now and he was all fired up. He didn't say anything, he just stood there wiping his hand on his ear and then on his pants.

"Let me explain what happened before you get us all into trouble." Bob said, standing his ground with an air of authority that surprised me.

"Why should I get in trouble?" He called back angrily. "I didn't do anything."

"That won't be true if you fight with Harry," Bob returned with undeniable logic.

Now everyone in the back of the bus was watching with interest. The activity hadn't reached to the front of the bus yet, but it seemed like it would if things didn't settle down quickly.

"What's your name?" Bob asked the boy.

After a short pause, the fellow answered, "Paul."

"Okay Paul. Just sit down for a moment and let me explain what happened. It was my fault and not Harry's. No one intended to do anything bad to you, " Bob continued. "It was an accident. Let me explain."

As Bob spoke to Paul, Bob pointed at Paul's seat and began to sit down in his own seat. That seemed to calm Paul down and he reluctantly sat as he pulled his shirt out of his pants and wiped his ear with the lower part of his shirt.

I was glad to see that things were settling down. As I was standing in the aisle, I began to become more worried about drawing attention from the front of the bus and Mr. Williams then from Paul. I was about to say something when Bob chimed in.

"Let Harry get back on his seat and I will explain things," Bob said to Paul. "Okay?"

Paul paused to think for a moment and then nodded his assent. I was a little hesitant to walk past him, but I had no choice. Now that Bob had negotiated a truce I had to go along with it. I expected Paul might try to trip me or push me, but he didn't. I climbed back up on the baggage and turned around to listen to Bob explain what had happened. To my surprise, Bob turned towards me and said, "Okay Harry, explain what happened."

At that, Paul looked from Bob's face to mine and back again. He seemed to be wondering if we were trying to put something over on him again. But Bob bit the bullet and said, "Paul, this is kind of embarrassing for me, so I'm going to have Harry tell you."

So, when both Bob and Paul had nodded to me I proceeded to share the story from the very beginning. As I warmed up to the tale I embellished here and there. By the time I was done, everyone in the back three rows was laughing uproariously. Even Paul was laughing.

When he realized that it really was a total accident, he took it with a good nature.

Bob apologized with sincerity and Paul accepted his apology. Soon the group was talking about boogers as if they were connoisseurs of the subject.

As the group began to carry on without me I started to reflect on what had just happened. Bob had surprised me with his willingness to stand up and take responsibility for his unintended actions. I know a lot of guys would have let Paul go at me. Bob also had spoken with more authority than I had expected. I recognized that as a leadership quality and wondered if that was something that he just had or if it was something that he had developed. My opinion of Bob rose quite a bit. I also realized that once again I had pigeon holed a person into being one way, when there was much more to them than I knew about.

Paul had been very good natured about the situation once he knew that no one was trying to hurt him. I thought that was big of him as well.

It also occurred to me that once again trouble had jumped up in front of me. Was I some kind of trouble magnet? This subject was going to take some more thought. I had to figure out if I was in some strange way causing these things to happen.

As my mind began to roll forward with the many complexities of what had happened we were all brought to attention by an announcement that came from the front of the bus. We were about to turn off the highway to visit the Four Corners. We were told that we should all prepare to be in four states at the same time.

That sounded interesting to everyone – which was no surprise since we had been sitting in the bus for hours with nothing to do. Boys started looking out the windows and cameras were being brought out of storage in order to capture the momentous moment. When we all realized that we were going to be able to get out of the bus and walk around for a while, we got really excited.

Chapter 6

As the bus rolled into a large parking lot all of the boys jumped up and started to jostle towards the front. There was no stewardess, like on an airplane, to warn us that we should "wait until the vehicle comes to a complete stop". Mr. Williams was busy driving and Mr. Davis was still asleep.

When the door of the bus opened all of the boys just streamed out like water from the floodgates of a dam. What we found once we had inspected the place was a typical tourist trap. There were only two things to do here: spend money on food and souvenirs, and take your picture with each foot and each hand in a different state.

Why everyone thought this was a cool thing to do I never quite understood, but that didn't stop me from getting my picture taken as I posed on the ground like a dog. With my left foot in Colorado, my right foot in Utah, my right hand in Arizona and my left hand in New Mexico, I raised my head up like man's best friend and smiled for the camera.

Once everyone was done with taking pictures and generally horsing around, we all headed back to the bus. At the bus we found that Mr. Williams and Mr. Davis had pulled out the makings for peanut butter and jelly sandwiches. Instantly the misadventures of the morning were forgotten and all of the boys built and ate their sandwiches with relish. With milk, water or soda to wash down the delicious meal, everyone was in a buoyant mood. Just being out of the bus and able to move around seemed like a great treat. Peanut butter and jelly made it a special event.

"Take your time boys," announced Mr. Williams. "We're going to stay here for a while so you guys can settle your stomachs and use the bathroom."

There was some laughter while everyone reviewed in their minds the events of the morning. "Good idea," shouted out one of the boys.

"Yah," called out another boy. "I think we are getting low on barf bags!" That brought some more laughter.

Soon all of the eating was done and the boys wandered around to see more of the trinkets that were being sold to tourists. A few boys bought postcards. One boy bought a little cedar box that said "Four Corners" on it. I didn't see anything of particular interest so I kept my money in my pocket.

After a while I wandered near a small table with some turquoise jewelry on it. There was an American Indian woman in a colorful skirt sitting at the table. Behind her was an older man who was also an American Indian. I had never seen American Indians except in the movies. Their skin was dark from the sun and they had wrinkles around their mouths and eyes. I didn't want to be rude, but I was fascinated by looking at them. So I moved away slightly to observe without being noticed.

I had always felt a kinship with various American Indian characters that I had seen in movies. I never for a minute believed that all "Redskins" were bad and all

"White Men" were good. And I didn't see any way the trampling and killing of women and children in a teepee village that I had seen in a movie could be justified by soldiers. Of course I wasn't around during those years in American history, but I had seen enough of life to feel confident that the stories from the past that we read in history books aren't always the true story.

I remembered how dignified and in harmony with nature the Chief of the Indians looked in one movie. When he sat bareback on his horse on the top of a hill as the wind blew through his long hair I thought that he was a strong and dignified human being. His skin color made no difference at all, except that I thought he was a handsome man.

As I watched the woman interact with a few tourists I noticed that she had a quiet manner. She wasn't trying to convince potential customers to spend their money, she was just offering the items on the table if anyone was interested.

It was hard to tell how old the man sitting behind her was. In some ways he looked ancient, in other ways - especially his eyes - he looked youthful and high spirited. As I watched him I tried to mentally reach out and feel what kind of person he was and what his life might be like. Then for the second time that morning, I got caught staring at someone.

When the American Indian man I was looking at turned his head and caught me looking at him, his expression didn't change one bit. He just looked back at me with a neutral face as if nothing was happening. Then as I continued to look, like a deer caught in the headlights of a car – panicked and fascinated at the same time – his face seemed to be reading mine. I felt as if his gaze was reaching into my mind to inspect what kind of person I was. Whatever he found there was apparently acceptable to him because after a moment, he smiled. I smiled back and we just stood their looking at each other.

In that moment I realized that this was a person like all people, with a life that has both hardship and joy. He was a fellow traveler on the journey of life and we had greeted each other from a point of truth inside ourselves. I was glad to meet him. I knew that my life was in some way better for our meeting.

Then, as if nothing at all had happened, he turned his head and looked away. The time had past, our paths were no longer traveling in the same direction. With his gaze now pointing away from me I felt freed from the intensity of the moment. I watched them at the table for a few more minutes and then made my way slowly back to the bus. The encounter had given me much to think about.

Not only did I feel that I had really met this man, but I wondered at how such a meeting could take place from a distance. We didn't talk, yet I felt that we had communicated. It had only been for a few moments, though it had seemed like a long time. Once again I wished that there was someone that I could talk to about this kind of thing. I wondered if I would ever meet someone who was wise enough to explain to me how and why these kinds of experiences happened.

Once back in the bus I thought for a long time about meeting that American Indian man and woman. Somehow the history that I had read about and seen in movies became more real. At the same time, the idea that a nation of people were brought to the edge of extinction as the result of creating the United States seemed somehow wrong. How our country could do such a bad thing wasn't clear to me. Here was another issue that would take more wisdom than I currently possessed.

When the bus started up and pulled away from the "Four Corners" I found that the place would hold more meaning for me than I would have guessed when we arrived. I hoped that the future would bring more opportunities to learn about and be with American Indians. How that might happen I had no idea, but I did hope that it would happen. Little did I know that I would soon be hiking on ancient trails and exploring the dwelling places of Indians that had lived many hundreds of years ago.

As the bus bounced its way down the road, all we boys knew about our destination was that it was a camp somewhere near Dolores, Colorado. We were never informed about how long it would take to get there or how many stops we might make along the way. For the next few hours we traveled west, then north, then west again and then finally south. During the southern leg of the journey we entered Mesa Verde National Park.

When the bus pulled into a campground Mr. Williams stood up and gave a little speech.

"Okay, guys," Mr. Williams started. "We are going to be camping here tonight. In the morning we will be doing some hiking and by late afternoon we will arrive at camp. We will be sleeping out under the stars tonight so get your sleeping bags out before it gets dark. We will be having dinner in about an hour, so from now until then you can wander around. Don't go too far and be sure that you use the buddy system. When dinner is ready we will honk the horn three times. Any questions?"

There weren't any questions, so we all jumped up to do something even if we didn't know what that something would be. Some of the boys wanted to dismantle the stack of baggage I had been sitting on, so I grabbed my backpack and sleeping bag off the stack and headed out of the bus. Once outside I leaned my stuff against one of the back tires of the bus and took a look around.

The campground was spacious enough. There weren't any other campers near us - which was probably just as well for them. Soon the area around the bus was littered with little piles of suitcases and sleeping bags. I wandered around for awhile wondering where I should sleep. I found a particularly green patch of ground and moved my things to it. Then I rummaged around to find my flashlight and toothbrush. Once that was done I did just what Mr. Williams told us not to do: I wandered off alone.

I didn't go far. I just wanted to get some private time away from all the other boys. I wasn't used to spending so much time in a group. I needed a rest from all of the mental interaction that took place just being around so many people. I found a tree to sit under, sat down with my back leaning against the trunk and tried to relax. I looked up and noticed that the trees here had lots of green on them. After the lack of greenery in the desert they stood out in my mind. I didn't know if the trees were natural to the area or if the Forest Service had planted and watered them to make it nice for campers. It was hot, but not as hot as the open desert that we had crossed the day before.

Once I had quieted down I noticed some birds who apparently lived in the neighborhood. I listened to them chirp for a while. I sat very still and eventually they either forgot I was there or just ignored me. They flitted from tree to tree in what seemed a happy rhythm of life. Some landed near me and I watched them peck at the ground while keeping an eye and ear out for predators.

I tried to imagine what it was like to live here, but I had no idea what the weather would be like during the winter months. I imagine that they got some food from the scraps that campers left behind, although I didn't know if campers came year round. The trees weren't very thick, it didn't seem like they would offer much shelter in a storm. The birds looked healthy to me, so I figured that whatever they did it must be working.

One thing that I liked about this place is that it was quiet. There was noise coming from the direction of the campground and all of the boys, but nature was quiet here. There was a feeling of peace and tranquility. I liked that and just sat drinking in the peace of the moment.

By the time the bus horn tooted three times to announce dinner I felt mentally refreshed. As the thought of food came to my mind my stomach announced that I was once again hungry. I had no idea what was for dinner, as I walked back to the bus I hoped that it was on my list of good things to eat.

Nearing the group I found everyone gathered around a campfire. On the fire there was a huge pot of spaghetti. Next to the coals there was some bread warming in aluminum foil. Mr. Williams was handing out paper plates and forks while Mr. Davis stirred the spaghetti. It amazed me that they had pulled a dinner together so quickly and without any of the conveniences of a kitchen. I was suitably impressed.

After I received my spaghetti I was even more impressed, it tasted really good. It reminded me of my camping experience in the boy scouts. It seems that food tastes better when it is cooked outside over a fire. Why that should be I don't know. But I was now realizing that it must be true. Plenty of food had been prepared, so everyone ate until their bellies bulged.

When we were done eating the mostly eaten pot of spaghetti was removed from the fire and some fresh logs were piled on top. Then to everyone's delight Mr.

Williams produced several bags of marshmallows. While I had been off on my own Mr. Williams had sent a group of boys to find roasting sticks. I grabbed a long skinny one from the pile and set about the delicate business of roasting the perfect marshmallow. For the next fifteen or twenty minutes we all gave ourselves up to the joys of sticky hot lumps of sugar.

There is an art to roasting marshmallows. I am not from the "catch it on fire" school of roasting. To me, a marshmallow should be roasted near coals with no flame. The distance and rotation should be carefully controlled so that an even brown can be achieved on the complete circumference of the marshmallow. Once the surface is properly browned it should be allowed to cool for a moment or two so that you don't damage the sensitive taste buds on the tongue. If you burn your mouth eating your first marshmallow you won't be able to enjoy the rest as much.

These are all-important aspects of quality marshmallow roasting. As I proceeded to roast my first marshmallow I noticed that many of the boys were too impatient to do the job right. They would just singe the surface with flames and get the marshmallow into their mouths as quickly as possible. One fellow couldn't seem to keep from dropping his marshmallow into the fire. He lost two into the fire before he got one to his mouth. Another boy burnt his tongue and had to get some water to relieve his discomfort.

When my marshmallow was perfectly brown all the way around I pulled it away from the fire. Several boys noticed me inspecting it while it cooled. They were quite impressed. I explained my technique and soon a number of guys were giving more attention to the quality of their roasting. I felt quite good about being able to help them on such an important subject.

When we were done with our dessert Mr. Davis produced a guitar. He had a pretty good voice and was obviously experienced in leading group singing. We then spent the next thirty minutes or so singing campfire songs. We sang songs like "She'll be Commin' Round the Mountain" ,"Clementine" , and we did "Row, Row, Row Your Boat" in a round. I had always enjoyed singing and so this was really fun.

We ended our singing with "Kumbya" and then Mr. Williams said an end of the day prayer. I wasn't used to hearing prayers. I wasn't really sure what to do, but I bowed my head and listened. Mr. Williams thanked God for all the good we had received that day. He asked God to bless our families and keep them safe. Then he asked God to bless us and keep us safe. That was followed with an Amen. I noticed that many - but not all - of the boys said Amen too. I was too surprised by the moment to say anything.

As we all dispersed to our sleeping areas I felt somewhat dazed by the unexpected spirituality of the moment. One moment we were singing songs and life was fun and easy-going, in the next moment God was involved. I had struggled with this before and didn't know quite what to do with it. In my heart I did believe in God, though I didn't know exactly why. It reminded me of my pact with God on the miniature golf course. I hadn't done much of anything about it since then.

As I climbed into my sleeping bag I wondered why life had to be so complicated. If I was supposed to understand stuff like God, why didn't someone just explain it to me? Or better yet, why didn't God just explain it to me Himself? Yes, that was better. I looked up at the star filled sky and mentally announced to God that if he wanted to chat, I was available.

That having been said, I decided that I was exhausted from the adventures of the day and closed my eyes. Soon I was asleep. Little did I know that I would be busy in my dreams.

Chapter 7

Who can say where dreams come from? Certainly not me. I just know that I had an incredible dream that night. Somehow I seemed to know that I was dreaming and once I was aware that I was dreaming I thought, "Cool. I think I'll have a look around."

I found myself in a very lush and beautiful forest during twilight. I wandered over to a small brook and tried to drink the water, but I couldn't get the water into my mouth; it wasn't clear to me why. Then I noticed a man upstream from me cupping his hands in the water and lifting it to his mouth. I followed his example and was able to drink myself; the water was cold and refreshing. When I looked up after taking a drink the man was gone.

I wandered further into the forest. After awhile I heard a sound in the distance but couldn't tell what it was. I kept trying to get closer to the sound but didn't seem to be making any progress. Then I saw a beautiful white horse with a long flowing mane that had some dark hairs mixed with the white hair. It was quite striking to see. The horse walked very gracefully, almost like it was in slow motion, but it wasn't. The horse looked at me and neighed. Then it walked in the direction of the noises that I was trying to reach.

I followed the horse for some time though I never seemed to get any closer even though I tried. The distant sounds did seem to be getting closer so I kept following. At one point the horse went around a large boulder and disappeared. When I got to the other side of the boulder the horse was gone, but I could hear clearly that there was a group of people not far away.

Strangely, I wasn't afraid. Even though this was very unusual I didn't have any feelings of potential harm. In fact, I felt very calm and peaceful. I walked for what seemed like a few more minutes and then noticed a light coming from a clearing in the forest. I approached to find a group of people sitting around a campfire. Now the only sound I could hear was the crackling of the flames.

The people around the fire were of different ages. There was a little boy of about five years old, a girl who looked around eight years old, two very old looking men, and three women who seemed to be middle aged. As I approached I tried to speak to them, but apparently they couldn't hear me. For some reason I couldn't tell how they were dressed, it was like that part of their bodies was kind of fuzzy. Their faces were clear and as I looked at them they reminded me of the American Indian man that I had met at Four Corners earlier in the day.

They didn't seem to mind my presence so I sat with them around the fire. Nothing was really happening, we were all just sitting there. I observed each person in turn, but got no direct response from their faces. When I got to the second old man I looked right into his eyes. As I did so he apparently recognized that someone was looking at him, though he didn't seem to know that it was me.

I kept looking at him and tried to talk to him. I could tell he couldn't hear me so I stopped. Then at one point the old man started to talk, I could see his lips moving but I couldn't hear him. Then he stopped talking and we both looked at each other.

After a few minutes of this I noticed his eyes suddenly got wider, it was like something had changed. A big smile came to his face and he started to nod his head up and down like he was saying yes. I raised my right hand and waved it back and forth at him. He raised his hand and waved it at me, smiling. I smiled back.

Then I had one of those moments that is both long and short - just as I had when looking into the eyes of the American Indian at Four Corners. It was as if a veil of distance had been lifted and I felt that I was meeting this person. It wasn't with words, it was a feeling. I could feel the presence of this man and apparently he could feel my presence. He started to talk. I couldn't hear the words, but I could feel that he was greeting me. I greeted him back and he smiled once again. Then as we looked into each other's eyes I went instantly from being in the forest looking into his face to waking up and sitting up in my sleeping bag.

I involuntarily gasped for breath. I was keenly aware that I had just awakened from a dream and remembered everything very clearly. I just couldn't figure out exactly what had happened and why it had happened. I had never had a dream like that. It was so real and I had been aware that I was dreaming. Yet it wasn't like being in the physical world.

Even though I wasn't afraid, I spoke to myself to confirm that I was awake and no longer dreaming. "Wow, that was interesting," I said to myself.

I looked around to see if anyone was up and about. Everything was quiet so I lay back down and pon-

dered what had happened. I didn't come to any firm conclusions but I did manage after some time to fall back
asleep. This time there were no conscious dreams to
wake me. I slept soundly until the chirping of a bird woke
me up. Even though the sun was still low in the sky it
wasn't cold, so I decided to get up.

After gathering up my things I made my way back
to the bus. Along the way I noticed that everyone else
was still sleeping. I stepped onto the bus and found there
were several boys that had decided to sleep in the bus.
It was when I was stepping off the bus that I had a thought
that might lead to some fun and/or trouble, depending
on how things went. At first I thought, "Come on Harry,
why stir things up?" And then I thought, "Why not stir things
up?"

So I silently put my plan into work.

I grabbed my sleeping bag and put it back where
I slept. Then I crept back to the bus making sure no one
saw me. If I was seen I would have to abandon the plan.
Once in the bus I grabbed a roll of toilet paper that had
been making the rounds as Kleenex. It had been used
to blow a few noses and wipe a few barfy faces, but
there was still plenty left to do the job that I had in mind. I
would have to work quickly. Once my plan had been
accomplished I made my way stealthily out of the bus
and back to my stuff, where I then sat waiting with keen
anticipation.

A few minutes later several boys were up and
wandering around the burnt out campfire. Then I saw Mr.
Williams approach the bus and made sure that he saw
me coming from my sleeping area. I poured it on pretty
thick by yawning loudly and acting like I had just woken
up as I stepped near him. It was all just too perfect.

As we approached the bus there was a sudden
yelling from one of the boys inside. Then another boy

yelled. After that bedlam took over and you couldn't tell what was going on. Mr. Williams ran quickly up to the bus and up the stairs. I followed close behind.

When we got to the top of the steps we found all five of the boys in the bus wrapped with toilet paper and trying to get out of their sleeping bags. They looked like reluctant mummies. They were yelling at each other, each accusing another of the dastardly deed.

"What's going on in here?" Mr. Williams shouted at the group.

They all turned to him and started shouting their explanations at the same time. It took all of my self-control to keep from laughing out loud.

"One at a time!" Mr. Williams called out pointing to Don Jones. "You first Don. What happened?"

"I don't really know," Don answered truthfully. "We all woke up with this toilet paper wrapped around us."

The other boys couldn't help chiming in with their, "Yes, me too!" Then accusations of guilt and exclamations of innocence started to fly around.

Before the boys could build up too much steam Mr. Williams asked, "Is anyone hurt?"

They all stopped and looked at each other. Then, like a choir, they chimed in with an unintentionally synchronized, "No."

"Well," said Mr. Davis with a chuckle, "you guys look like mummies. "

Then they all looked at each other for a moment and started to laugh. Once the laughter started I felt free to cut loose on my own. I laughed heartily until I noticed that I was the only one still laughing. Then in the back of my mind there was a little voice saying, "Oops!"

Suddenly the whole group was looking at me with suspicion since I had a reputation for doing this sort of thing. Mr. Williams looked at me with intense scrutiny.

"Are you responsible for this Fruitgarden?" Mr. Williams asked accusingly.

"Why would you think that Sir?" I replied, putting on my most innocent face.

"Because you are here laughing your head off," Mr. Williams replied logically.

"You are here too and I do believe you were laughing," I commented with an innocent inflection. "And besides, it is pretty funny." I gave a kindly chuckle and looked at the mummified boys to make my point.

He turned to look at them himself and couldn't help laughing. Then the boys all looked at themselves and started to laugh again. Soon more boys came streaming on the bus to see what was going on. Then the word spread like wildfire and the next thing I knew the five boys were dancing in the back of the bus like a mummy chorus line to rows of benches that had filled with delighted sleepy eyed boys.

During our breakfast of more cold cereal and then later on as we filled the bus with our baggage I overheard some boys talking. There was apparently a pretty strong rumor going around that I had been responsible for the mummy incident. I observed with a smile that there was lots of speculation, but no proof. A few boys who had missed the whole affair were very upset about missing it. They requested others to relay what had taken place, and as often happens, exaggerations quickly grew the story beyond all truth. Should an interviewer from a prominent newspaper come along to get the story from one of these kids I am sure that the next morning's headline would be something like: "Innocent Prank Causes Near Death Experience" or "Heartless Jokester Causes Colossal Suffering".

All in all I considered it one of my better escapades. No one got hurt, everyone was having a good time, and no one knew for sure if I had been the culprit. Yes, I had the feeling it was going to be a good day.

Chapter 8

After breakfast we jumped into the bus for a short ride to a ranger station further south in the park. Upon arrival our group was met by a park ranger. Soon Ranger Bill was telling us that fourteen centuries of history are displayed at Mesa Verde National Park. The Park was established by Congress in 1906. Mesa Verde is the first national park set aside to preserve the works of aboriginal Americans.

Ranger Bill started to drone on about the different sub-mesas having different names and how many visitors came each year. With each new fact that meant nothing to me I started to tune out his little talk. I still had no idea what was going on here and Ranger Bill wasn't helping. As I looked at the other kids in our group I could see that I was not the only one losing interest.

I was just about to start looking for alternative entertainment when a few of Ranger Bill's words broke through to me. He was saying, " The earliest inhabitants of the area were nomadic peoples who lived in the area from at least 10,000 B.C.. "

That was kind of interesting, but it was the next part that got my attention.

"So today," He went on, "we will be hiking down to some cliff dwellings that were built between A.D. 450 and A.D. 1300."

It was the hiking down part that caught my interest. I was beginning to realize that we were about to visit an ancient village that was built in a cave on the side of a cliff. Why didn't he just say that in the first place?

Ranger Bill kept talking about stuff like primary crops of corn, beans and squash. Then he would throw in domesticated turkeys and wild plants. Finally I couldn't stand it any more, I threw my hand up in the air to ask a question.

Ranger Bill seemed pleased that someone was interested enough to ask a question. "Yes," He called out to me. "You have a question?"

"Yes, I do." I replied. "When do we get to start climbing?"

My question caused the group to start laughing and Mr. Williams jumped in with a hearty, "Okay guys, pipe down."

To Ranger Bill's credit, his face only deflated for a millisecond. He really had the "don't overreact" attitude down pat. I had seen many seasoned teachers falter in situations like this.

"In just a few minutes," He replied with a smile that actually seemed partially sincere. Then – I suppose because he wore a uniform – he re-established his authority by droning on for another ten minutes as if I hadn't asked the question at all. I had to admire that in a way - even though it was slightly irritating.

Finally he announced that we were ready to proceed.

We hiked for awhile along the side of the road and then headed west. When we got to the edge of a large valley it became apparent that we were on top of one of the mesas that Ranger Bill had been talking about. The valley was pretty large and quite beautiful, it wasn't nearly as big as the Grand Canyon which basically defined the words "Big Canyon", still, this was a pretty cool place.

After being properly informed about safety issues – I'm sure there was a long list of official park regulations on this subject – we started to climb down a steep trail that went over the eastern edge of the canyon.

As soon as we went over the edge of the canyon I felt that we had left civilization as we know it far behind. I tried to imagine that I was a member of the ancient tribe coming home after being out looking for food. When I put myself in that mental frame of mind I could feel my senses becoming keener. I was intensely aware of the sun rising in the sky. I could smell the odors of the trail dust mixing with the aromas of the plants and bushes that we passed. I heard, but didn't see, the cry of a bird somewhere above us. It seemed to be announcing our arrival.

The trail was steep enough that we had to use our hands for climbing down. I could feel with my fingers the texture of the time worn trail. It occurred to me that this wasn't a place that you wanted to be wandering around at night in the dark.

A couple of the boys started to get nervous about the steepness of the trail, but they were boxed in by boys above and below, so they had to keep going. Since they were going so slow I stopped and took notice of my surroundings.

Being under the rim of the mesa gave a very different impression of the environment. We had descended maybe fifty yards down into the canyon and we were looking out over the valley. We could see a riverbed below and large caves in the wall along the other side of the valley. The caves looked very…well, I had trouble finding the right words to describe them. Words like cool, neat, amazing, incredible, all of these words were good, but they didn't capture the feeling that I was getting from being here.

I decided that I would have to come up with my own word, I wasn't about to let the English language limit me. As my mind wandered over possible words I tried to open myself up mentally to how the inhabitants of this place might have viewed their world. I could visualize them as seeing it as ancient, beautiful and holy. So I called it "Holificent". Yes, this was a truly Holificent place.

Once we got to the bottom of the trail we traversed along a very narrow path with a steep drop on the downhill side. Then we walked through a very narrow gap between some large boulders. Once past this narrow entrance the cave and its dwellings became visible. It was much bigger than I expected. There were two story mud and rock dwellings with little rooms in the back of the cave, a spring with fresh water, and a kiva – which is a round covered hole in the ground used for meetings and as a sweat lodge. There was even some open space for people to gather and do whatever those people did in those days. Probably the parents spent a lot of time keeping their kids from falling off the edge into valley floor far below.

We spread out to explore the cave which was large enough to house thirty or fourty people. Ours was the only group there so we didn't have to worry about disturbing other tourists. After inspecting most of the cave I took my turn climbing down into the kiva. I sat down on the dirt and tried to imagine the men of the village discussing the day's hunt or the expectations of the crops that they grew up on the mesa. There were probably turkeys running around free in the cave village, so the sounds of their gobbling would carry in the air.

At one point I found myself alone in the kiva. I closed my eyes and tried to mentally reach out to those ancient cliff dwellers. As I sat there listening and looking inside myself I remembered the dream that I had just last night. As I visualized the face of the old man in the dream I felt touched by his spirit. I wasn't sure, but it seemed like I was getting the message that the old man and the people that I had seen in the dream had something to do with the cave dwellers.

This was a little too weird even for me. I opened my eyes to find John Wilson staring at me from the other side of the kiva. I had known him since the second grade. We had done a few things together over the years, but we weren't what you would call close friends. He tended to hang around with guys that didn't like me too much.

"What's wrong with you Harry?" He asked with some derision in his voice.

"Nothing," I replied, somewhat surprised by his sudden appearance. I had no idea how long he had been watching me.

"At first I thought you had fallen asleep, but now you look like you have seen a ghost." The boy said while scrutinizing my face.

I was tempted to say that, well, yes it appears I have seen a ghost! But I knew that not only would I not be believed, I would be teased mercilessly for the rest of the trip. So I kept my experiences to myself and just said, "Oh, is that what you are? I thought you looked a little strange."

The next thing I knew John was standing up in a threatening manner. Great, all I need now is to have a fight in the ancient kiva.

"Whoa, John. I'm sorry. But it is a little spooky here isn't it?" I said to try and shift from fighting to talking.

John stopped to think for a moment. Apparently he didn't really want to fight. He was just a bit edgy as well. So he said, "Yes, it is kind of spooky here. Do you think there really are ghosts here?"

Now that he was moving away from the fighting direction and into the talking direction I felt like I could relax. "Let me put it this way, John, if there is such a thing as ghosts, I would be surprised if there weren't a few of them hanging around here," I replied sincerely.

He nodded in agreement as he looked around in all directions to confirm that there was nothing he could see in the way of ghosts. As he looked around another boy climbed down into the kiva. With more people in the small space it seemed less likely that there would be room for ghosts, I think that was reassuring to John.

I took the arrival of more boys as my cue to climb out of the kiva. My next destination was a place where I could sit and look out over the valley to the cliffs on the other side. I found a small spot right near the edge of the drop-off and sat down to enjoy the view.

As I looked across the valley at the other caves I started to imagine how this area could have been filled with people who lived in different cave communities. I wondered if they all got along with each other or if they would have fights. I imagined that they would be territorial about their cave and their part of the valley. Then I remembered that Ranger Bill had talked about the access trails as being designed to discourage unwanted visitors and easy to defend. Then it hit me that in all these hundreds of thousands of years mankind hadn't improved much except for the heating and plumbing. Intertribal warfare struck me as not much different than gang warfare or war in general.

That led me to thinking that it would sure be nice if people could learn to work together for a common good instead of fighting each other. I wasn't sure if that was possible since it wasn't a common part of recorded history, but it did seem like a good idea. I tried to come up with a reason that it couldn't work. Like the idea that you can't travel to the stars because there is no such thing as faster than light travel. Then it occurred to me that there used to be no such thing as flying in the air – unless of course, you were a bird. The Wright Brothers had taken care of that, so maybe someone would discover how to travel faster than light. And if that could be done, maybe people could learn to live in harmony with each other. And....Whew! That was a lot of deep thinking.

Responsibility for the evolution of mankind was a pretty heavy task. I decided that maybe I should just enjoy the view. So I watched some birds fly, some insects crawl in the dirt and tossed a small rock off the edge to watch it tumble down the hill. Boy was tossing that rock a mistake!

No sooner had the rock left my hand then Ranger Bill was standing over me like an angry mother hen protecting her chick.

"What do you think you are doing?" Ranger Bill said sternly.

I was so taken aback by Ranger Bill's tone that I didn't know what to say. All I was doing was sitting on the ground looking out and tossing a little....Oh, no. We weren't supposed to toss rocks here. All the rocks were part of the "ancient archeological site". I had unintentionally broken a cardinal rule about not disturbing such places. It was a little rock, but that was no excuse. I decided that Ranger Bill had a point.

Unfortunately, most of the kids and Mr. Williams as well, were now watching with relish to see what would happen next. Once again Harry Fruitgarden was in the middle of controversy. I stood up and faced Ranger Bill. Out of the corner of my right eye I could see a boy watching with fascination like when you watch a snake eat a mouse. In the back of my mind I couldn't help sending him a, "Hope you enjoy the show!"

I think Ranger Bill was expecting a denial or excuse of some kind. In any case, I thought he also might consider this an opportunity to get me back for my question earlier in the day. But I saw surprise in his face when looking him right in the eyes I said, "I just realized what I did. I shouldn't have thrown that rock over the edge. I just wasn't thinking about it at the time. But that is no excuse, this is a great place and it needs to be preserved. I am really sorry."

It took Ranger Bill a moment to fully absorb that I was taking responsibility for what I had done. I understood the infraction and I was contrite. I could see in his face that he was registering all of the essential elements of proper decorum at this point. Most importantly, I think he saw that I really meant what I said. I wasn't acting just to get out of being in trouble.

"Okay son," He said finally. "I appreciate that you understand why it is so important that we preserve these sites. This won't happen again?" He asked.

"No sir," I responded. "It won't."

"Okay then," He said looking me in the eye again to see if I meant it. Apparently he saw that I did because he then turned away to check on the rest of the group.

I was just recovering from the intensity of the encounter with Ranger Bill when Mr. Williams walked up to me. "Oh no," I thought, here we go again. But Mr. Williams surprised me.

"You are quite a character Harry Fruitgarden," He said, patting me on the shoulder. Then without another comment he walked away.

I wasn't exactly sure what he meant by that and I was glad that he kept moving. I really didn't want to do any more mental sparing with adults until I had a chance to relax. Things had been moving pretty intensely lately, there was a lot going on in my head. It was interesting to have an exciting life, but also exhausting. I decided to see if I could be invisible for a while, although that might be a big challenge in itself. Could I not draw attention to myself between now and when we get back on the bus?

In spite of my good intentions, apparently the answer to my question is no. But I didn't find that out until we were climbing our way back up the cliff.

Chapter 9

My strategy for invisibility was that I would just quietly hang around in the background of the group. I didn't wander off on my own, nor did I enter into one of the small sub groups of boys that hung out together. Kids were still milling about the cave when Ranger Bill announced that it was time to head back up to the top of the mesa.

I decided to get in the middle of the line as we left the cave, figuring: What could be more invisible then being in the middle? I couldn't have been more wrong.

Once we were out of the cave we headed up the steep trail. It was going slowly because we had to use hands and feet to climb. As I followed the boy in front of me I gave him a little room so that he wouldn't kick rocks and dirt in my face. Not too far up the trail I found that we took a fork that led us up a different trail then the one we had come down.

A couple of minutes later I found the boy in front of me stopped on the trail. I looked up to see what had stopped him and found that the line ahead of us was climbing large wooden pole ladders. I nodded with approval at the idea. They would be easier and safer to climb then the dirt trail that we had come down and besides, it looked like fun.

Apparently the boy in front of me didn't agree with my assessment. He had stopped and was looking somewhat panicked as he looked up the ladder that seemed to go on forever. I looked around to see if Mr. Williams or Mr. Davis were around. With a limited view above and almost no view below, I couldn't see how far away they were. I knew Ranger Bill was at the front of the line so there was no way he could help. I figured that I would have to see what I could do to get things moving in the upward direction.

The boy had dark hair, a friendly face, and was just a little bigger than myself. I didn't know him so I asked, "Hey, what is your name?"

He responded with a nervous, "I'm Hank."

"Hi Hank," I responded. "I'm Harry."

"Yes I know," He said with a little smile. "You're the guy that toilet papered those guys in the bus."

"That is just a rumor," I said quickly, but not denying it. "There is no proof whatsoever that I did that."

"Yes, I know," He commented back with a knowing smile. "But we all know you did it." There wasn't much I could say to that. Contrary to the belief of many adults, it had been my observation that most kids aren't lacking in the capacity to know what is going on in life. They often see to the core of the things well before teachers and parents.

Our conversation seemed to be calming him a little so I decided to ask in my most soothing voice, "So what seems to be the problem here?"

"I am afraid to climb ladders," He responded as we both looked up at the very tall ladder in front of us.

"That is not good," I responded with a light-hearted chuckle.

Hank apparently took my reaction with the good-natured intention that I had made it and responded as we continued to look up, "No, it is not good."

As we stood there silently pondering the situation we watched the line in front of us climb farther and farther away, while behind us we started to hear grumbles about what was holding back the line. The trail was so narrow that no one could pass. I became aware that I could smell the earthy aroma of the dry brush nearby and started to hear the buzzing of insects as they went about their business. It occurred to me that nature was always at work no matter what kind of trouble people found themselves in.

My reflections on life and nature were interrupted by the boy below us. He called up, "Mr. Williams wants to know what the hold up is!"

Apparently the grapevine communication system was working in the up direction. I said to the boy, "Tell him that Hank is nervous about climbing the ladder."

Unfortunately the grapevine in the down direction wasn't working as well as in the up direction. At the time I had no idea that - like in the post office game where you send a message from ear to ear and it ends up different at the end then it started in the beginning – my message would be translated by the time that it got to Mr. Williams into: Harry is causing problems on the ladder!

I turned my attention back to Hank and his situation. I had some sympathy for him. This reminded me of the first time I had climbed the fence behind the handball court at school, it had been pretty scary. I figured climbing fences and ladders wasn't much different.

"So why don't you like ladders?" I asked Hank.

"I'm not sure," He responded honestly. "I just don't like them."

As Hank spoke I reached out inside my mind for a solution. Amazingly, a moment later an idea occurred to me. I asked Hank, "Have you ever climbed up into a tree house?"

"Yes," He answered.

"Have you ever climbed up the ladder to a bunk bed?" I asked again.

"Yes," He answered again.

"Well then Hank, it occurs to me that it isn't ladders that bothers you," I told him.

Hank looked at me with a question on his face. "What do you mean?" He asked.

"I mean that climbing isn't the problem," I answered. "You don't mind climbing ladders."

"Then what is my problem?" He asked sincerely.

"Well, I'm not sure exactly, but I know it isn't climbing ladders," I said. "It might be about heights. Are you afraid of heights?"

"Not that I know of," He answered.

"Have you ever fallen off something high?" I asked.

"Not that I know of," He answered again.

As we talked my mind was looking around inside my head for a solution to this situation, I knew there must be one but I wasn't sure what it was. Then once again, like a light going on in a dark room, a solution just appeared to me. I tried not to smile as I pushed forward with what I hoped would work.

"Well, It seems to me that you have what I call an invisible fear, something that you can't see is bothering you." I announced with confidence.

Hank paused to think for a moment and then said, "That makes sense. What do I do about it?"

I put on my best pondering face even though I knew exactly what I was going to say. I really wanted him

70

to believe me so I put both confidence and sincerity into my voice, "Well Hank, the solution is that you have to close your eyes."

"You are out of your mind!" He shouted back at me.

I was expecting this so I answered back right away. "Yes, I know, many people have said that to me before. But listen to what I have to say before you make a decision. You said that you agree about the invisible fear idea right?"

He nodded his head up and down hesitantly, but with an affirmative response.

"Well," I went on, "If you close your eyes, you can't see your invisible fear."

"What does that mean? He asked, like I had just spoken a foreign language.

"It means that you've climbed other ladders in the past because you couldn't see anything to be afraid of. That means you can climb this ladder if you don't see anything to be afraid of. So if you close your eyes, you won't see anything to be afraid of," I said, once again radiating confidence in the hopes it would bolster my argument.

"Well, that makes sense," he said, "but…"

I cut him off before he could justify disagreeing with me. I said quickly, "Let's just try it." And I turned him towards the ladder hoping that he wouldn't stop to think any more about what he was going to do.

"You can see how far the rungs of the ladder are apart, all you have to do is feel for the next one. I will let you know when you get to the top." I told him. "Just close your eyes and start climbing. Think of it as climbing up to a tree house."

Hank seemed hesitant, but he placed his hands on the ladder and closed his eyes.

"I'm right here behind you," I told him. "I will tell you what to do if you aren't finding the rungs to grab or step on."

To my relief, Hank actually started to climb. At first he was hesitant and I had to tell him where to put a hand or foot as he proceeded. By the time he was up three or four rungs he was building confidence.

"It is working," He called down with his eyes closed and a smile on his face. "This is fun," He announced. The next thing I knew he was picking up speed and I had to concentrate on keeping up with him.

I told Hank when he was near the top. I got nervous when he opened his eyes and looked down at me, but he had a big grin on his face. He was no longer afraid. Something about going up in spite of his fear had released his fear. He was bursting with jubilation at his victory over fear.

At the top of the ladder we found another ladder. Hank eagerly started up the second ladder with his eyes open and a spring in his steps. It didn't take too long for us to find ourselves up at the top and surrounded by a group of kids who wanted to know what had taken so long.

Hank blurted out the story with enthusiasm and soon some of the boys were patting me on the back for helping Hank out. Even Ranger Bill came over to me and said, "That was quick thinking son, good job." And then he thrust out his hand for me to shake, which I did even though I didn't see what the big deal was.

Boys from below started to appear and get the story as it buzzed around the group. I noticed a few of them fell into silence instead smiling; the reason for their silence soon became apparent.

When Mr. Williams finally got to the top from his position at the back of the line he marched straight over to me and started in on how I was always causing trouble. Fortunately for me and Mr. Williams, Ranger Bill interrupted Mr. Williams and took him aside for a little chat. As they talked I watched Mr. Williams' face go through a series of conflicting facial expressions. A few moments later I was the recipient of a public apology by Mr. Williams.

"It has come to my attention, Mr. Fruitgarden," He spoke contritely, "That I was misinformed about what was taking place on the ladders. I was told you were causing trouble, not that you were helping to avoid it. I apologize for misunderstanding the situation. And I want to thank you for helping Hank get up the ladders."

Once again an adult was sticking out their hand to shake mine. I stepped forward and shook Mr. William's hand. Then I was surrounded by a bunch of the boys who all wanted to shake my hand and congratulate me. As their faces bobbed with animated smiles all I could think was, "So much for being invisible!"

Chapter 10

By the time we had walked back to the bus I had managed to retreat back into invisibility. I walked alone trying to figure out why everyone had made such a big deal out of the whole thing. All I did was give Hank an alternative way of looking at his situation. I hadn't even really thought of it, the idea had just popped into my mind!

It all seemed kind of hollow to me. First everyone hates me. Then everyone loves me. What am I, a ping pong ball? And how did the opinions of others really affect my view of myself? Was I supposed to feel good about myself when others liked me and feel bad about myself when they didn't? I didn't see how it was a very good idea to rely on the opinions of others as to how I should feel about myself, yet lots of people depend on others for their sense of self-value. What I really wanted to know was why people never talk about this kind of stuff? Is everyone just supposed to figure all this out by themselves?

Since I knew I wasn't going to be able to answer my own question I decided to table the subject for awhile. Upon arriving back at the bus the peanut butter and jelly was brought out again. Some of the boys grumbled, but

I love peanut butter and jelly so I just made a big thick sandwich and enjoyed every bite.

After lunch and a stomach-settling break we got on our way. Today was the day we would arrive at camp. We were all excited about both arriving at camp and getting out of the bus. Which was the greater anticipation would be hard to say, everyone was pretty tired of being on the bus.

It didn't take us long to find ourselves in the high desert that surrounds Cortez, Colorado. At 6,200 feet I thought there would be more greenery, but it was definitely dry. To the north and east we could see the San Juan Mountain range which was our destination. Once we had passed through Cortez we started to wind our way up higher into the mountains: desert turned into pine, cedar and aspen trees. There were green meadows and after awhile we came upon the Dolores River. About forty miles later we passed through Dolores, Colorado. With just over twenty miles to go, the road followed the Dolores River. We could see clear waters and rapids flowing downstream through forest and meadow, it was really beautiful.

As the road climbed in elevation the air cooled and the fresh clean smells of nature in the mountains came wafting in through the windows. We saw horses and cows grazing in the deep green meadows. We saw birds flying high in the sky. We couldn't see them, but we guessed there were lots of fish swimming in the river. The excitement began to build until some of the boys were literally bouncing up and down in their seats.

The scenery was so picture perfect that my mind started to salivate with the possibilities the way a hungry person's mouth begins to get started before the food actually arrives. The further we got up that road the farther I felt that I was from my life in the city. I could feel all of the tensions that I held in my body and mind from the daily challenges of getting along at home and at school slipping away.

By the time we turned right down a dirt driveway and over a wooden bridge that crossed the Dolores River - which ran right in front of the Lodge – I felt like a person that had been on a long trip. It wasn't a long trip to go to a new and exotic place, but a long trip that would end in arriving at home. The sign that announced our arrival at the Circle H Ranch seemed to have special meaning to me. It might have been that H is the first letter in my name, but I felt like it was more than that. In some strange way I felt that I was arriving at a new life. Here I had the potential to become any kind of person I wanted to be. I wondered: What would that person be like?

If any of the other kids were feeling this way I saw no signs of it. All the boys were up and out of their seats, grabbing all of their belongings so that they could race out of the bus as quickly as possible. Since I was in the very back of the bus I didn't see any reason to try and rush things. I just lay there looking out the window, trying to imagine what the summer would bring.

Once we were stopped in front of the lodge Mr. Williams made an announcement. "Okay boys," He called out, trying to be heard over all the noise everyone was making. "Hey, guys! Listen up!"

Gradually everyone quieted down. Mr. Williams tried again to make his announcements. "Okay, here is what we are going to do. We will be splitting up into two groups of twenty. Group one will stay in Bunkhouse One and Group Two will stay in Bunkhouse Two. I will now call out the names of group one."

Then Mr. Williams called out twenty names. Each boy was congratulated by the group as if they had won a prize. The list didn't include my name.

"Everyone else is in group two," Mr. Williams announced. After looking at his wristwatch Mr. Williams went on, "It is now 4 o'clock. Get your stuff settled in the bunkhouse and have a look around the place. The supper bell will ring at half past five. When you hear it come to the dinning hall in the main lodge. Just don't go out of sight of the lodge or the bunkhouse. Any questions?"

One boy in a red plaid shirt with scruffy brown hair called out a question right away, "Can we go fishing?"

"You can if you think you have time," answered Mr. Williams. Anywhere around the bridge is fine. But remember; don't go out of sight of the lodge."

There were no more questions so Mr. Williams jumped off the bus to get out of the way while forty crazed boys tried to get out behind him all at the same time. Mr. Davis opened the door in the very back of the bus to help get the baggage out. That was pretty convenient for me, I just slid out the back, avoiding all the congestion in the front of the bus. And since I had my bags on top of the pile, I was able to move quickly towards the bunkhouse.

It didn't take me long to find Bunkhouse Two. When I walked in the door I found one open room with ten beds lined up on each side. In the very back was a door that I guessed would lead to a bathroom. Since the door to the bunkhouse was in the middle of the long building, I decided to head towards the opposite end that had the bathroom: I didn't like the idea of guys parading past my bed all the time.

A couple of boys had beaten me to the bunkhouse, but they chose the first two bunks they could find, so I had my choice and decided on one in the very corner of the room. It seemed the most private - if you could claim any kind of privacy in a room with twenty guys.

Soon the room was filling up with boys carrying their sleeping bags and suitcases or backpacks. Some of the boys had fishing poles and you had to be careful around them or you might get one of your eyes poked out. There was lots of excitement and shouting going on. Kids were pulling all kinds of stuff out of their suitcases. I saw one boy bring out a small teddy bear and tuck it quickly under his pillow, I turned my eyes quickly away so he wouldn't know that I had seen it. That looked like a pretty private thing to me.

Once my sleeping bag was laid out and my suitcase was tucked under my bed, I decided to go out and do some exploring. I headed out toward the bridge and the river.

Just 50 yards in front of the main lodge of the Circle H Ranch was the Dolores River. The river was around thirty feet wide when it went under the wooden bridge that allowed access to the ranch from the main road. As the bridge crossed the river it was about ten feet above the undulating surface of the water.

I walked out onto the bridge and leaned on the wood railing that protected people from falling in. Looking upstream I could see lots of pine and cedar trees lining the riverbanks. The river upstream was more shallow than by the bridge, I could see rocks sticking out above the water's surface. There were some small rapids where the course of the river had focused its attention between some larger rocks.

As I stood on the bridge I took in a deep breath of the mountain air, it was clean and fresh. The day was warm but not hot like the desert that we had crossed. There were a few clouds in the sky to add a contrasting white to the brilliant blue that seemed to have no limit to its depth. As I stood there trying to take in all of the aliveness that seemed to be bursting from every blade of grass, the trees, the river and the sky, I instinctively knew that I was going to really like this place.

I had always loved the *Adventures of Tom Sawyer* and *Huckleberry Finn*. This seemed like the perfect place for me to embrace nature's beauty the way they did. It then occurred to me that those two great lovers of life took in the very texture of the places they traveled through with more than just their eyes and ears, they also took in life through their feet. How did they do this? They went barefoot!

As soon as the air hit my toes I knew that I had made the right decision. It was like my toes had been in prison and now they were free. They were very happy with this turn of events and sent me messages of pleasure. I wiggled my toes and smiled, joining their happiness with my happiness.

Once I had enjoyed this newfound toe freedom for awhile I turned my attention back to the river. I crossed the bridge to the downstream side and looked over the edge. After going beneath the bridge the water entered a deep pool and appeared to slow down. As I watched the swirling patterns of the current I saw a fish swim up past the surface of the water to catch some dinner. The fish's mouth was wide open as it broke through the surface and then it came down with a big flopping sound that made me smile.

My smile faded when two boys came running up to the bridge with fishing poles. I instantly remembered my fishing experience at Crescent Lake with the Boy Scouts. I had caught a fish and watched it die. I had a lot of trouble reconciling my love for nature and all animals with the idea of killing and eating innocent creatures. When you buy meat in a store you don't have to look into the eyes of the animal you are eating and watch it die.

The boys with the fishing poles were very excited. They hurried to prepare their hooks with bait and get them in the water. I knew I couldn't stop them from fishing. I really didn't feel that I should try. I just didn't want to participate in it, so I moved off the bridge and down towards the edge of the water.

As I walked off the bridge and stepped onto some gravel my newly freed feet began to protest. After a few steps they started to send questioning messages up my legs, like: Ouch! And, Oww! Is this barefoot idea really as good as we thought?

In order to give some consolation to my rebelling feet I gingerly made my way towards the river. The sandy mud on the edge of the water was wonderfully squishy. When the dark mixture squeezed between my toes I had to laugh. I then spent the next few minutes stomping around to enjoy that squishy sensation. It was wonderful.

When I was done in the mud I stepped into the cold water of the river. My feet seemed unsure about how they felt. On one hand they were enjoying the rush of sensations and the texture of the riverbed. On the other hand, the water was pretty cold.

After a few minutes my feet got used to the cold and decided that they were fully enjoying the river experience. I pulled the legs of my blue jeans up so that I could go a little deeper into the water. As the water rushed by I couldn't help grinning, it just made me happy.

At the time I didn't realize that my current happy mood would be short lived. I was so concentrated on enjoying the water that I wasn't paying any attention to what was going on around me. That was a mistake.

Chapter 11

It is understandable that after two days of confinement on the bus everyone would be itching to get out and do something fun and exciting. I myself was feeling much better after just a few minutes of freedom to explore camp. But my explorations were of nature, some of the other boys seemed to think that exploring the youthful practice of picking on others was a pleasant pastime.

As I was fully absorbed in water, mud, and toe wiggling, I didn't pay any attention to what was going on behind me: that is often a mistake in life. It definitely was for me at this moment in particular. I clearly remember looking down through the clear water at my feet when I was pushed from behind with sufficient force to quickly find myself face down in the water. I didn't have to look to know that a boy had pushed me; some things in life are just instantly understandable to boys. My mind accepted the truth without question, the only thing that I needed to decide quickly was what to do about it.

One thing that I have noticed about bullies is that they hate to be laughed at. If you can turn the tables on them by making them look silly for their own actions, that is much better than actually beating them in a fight. The key is to quickly come up with a way to do so from a safe distance.

Since I was now in the water I knew I was pretty safe. So as I picked myself up and turned towards my assailant all the while my mind raced to come up with just the right comment to make. As luck would have it, just as I saw who my cowardly attacker was I also saw Mr. Williams come out of the lodge and head our way. I could see that Mr. Williams was looking around and not at the river, so I figured I had enough time to work a plan that had just presented itself to my mind.

Eric Winston isn't really all that big, his bushy brown hair and thick features give the impression that he is bigger than he actually is. The other thing that makes him seem bigger is the way he acts, he is a classic "stay out of my way or I'll get you" kind of guy. I am not sure why, but he just seems to be one of those people who is prickly. He is hard to be around without getting stuck by one of the thorns of his negative attitude.

As soon as I saw him I knew he was the one who had pushed me. I could also tell because he was pointing at me and laughing. He turned back to look at two of his minions and they laughed as well. Once he could see that his pals were with him he turned again towards me and increased the volume of his auditory display while he flailed his arms around.

His pose inspired me to do the same. So I flailed my arms around a little and then pointed at him and started to laugh. At first he didn't get that I was doing a parody of him. He eventually figured it out and responded with, "Yah, right Fruitgarden. Nice try, I got you good. You deserve to get all wet for all the trouble you cause."

"Well, I may deserve it, but you are the one who is going to get it," I answered back with more confidence than he expected. He had no idea what I thought was about to happen.

Eric spent a moment trying to figure out if he had missed something. When He couldn't think of anything he responded aggressively, "Oh, yah? What are you going to do about it?" He then stepped towards me with exaggerated menace.

As I watched him it added to the reality of my laughter, he really did look funny. Of course, this made him even madder so he looked even more funny. I couldn't help thinking that this was just too perfect. I looked Eric right in the eyes and gave him my very best smile, twitched my eyebrows up and down to give accent to my plan, and then jerked my face quickly into a mask of utter pain and dejection.

Eric started to smile, thinking that he had over-powered me with his threats. Then I turned my gaze past him to Mr. Williams who was just arriving within earshot of us. I started to trudge out of the water, putting all of my theatrical talents to work. I slouched, limped and gener-ally looked miserable as I made my way out of the water.

When Mr. Williams caught sight of me he ran the last fifteen yards towards me. Putting an arm on my shoul-der Mr. Williams asked, "Are you alright Fruitgarden?"

I hesitated for a moment – knowing that there is nothing like a nice long pause to create additional dra-matic affect. I also took that pause to turn my face away from Mr. Williams and look back at Eric with a quick smile and wink. Eric's face registered shock and then the knowledge that something bad was about to happen. Suddenly the tables were turned and he felt the victim.

"Well, I think I'm okay," I replied in a halting voice. I even coughed a little as if I had almost drowned.

"What happened here?" Mr. Williams asked look-ing around.

No one said anything. Eric and his two friends just stood there like statues.

"Come on, what happened?" Mr. Williams asked again looking at me.

"Well," I said as if I was reluctant to speak. "Eric seems to think that I deserve to be dunked in the water with all my clothes on."

Eric and his little group went stiff. They knew they were in serious trouble.

"Did you guys push Harry in the water?" Mr. Williams asked.

It really was pitiful, I almost felt sorry for them. Eric started a half-hearted denial by swinging his head slowly left and right, but his two cohorts didn't hesitate, they both pointed like twin marionettes at Eric. "He did it!" They announced in unison as if they had been waiting for just such a moment all their lives.

Mr. Williams looked right at Eric and said, "What happened Mr. Winston?"

Eric was so dumbfounded by this turn of events that he couldn't come up with anything to say. He just stood there shrugging his shoulders and looking stupidly guilty. If I hadn't just been pushed in the water by him I might actually have started to feel sympathy for him.

"Okay boys, you will now go back to your bunks until supper," Mr. Williams said like a judge who has pronounced guilt and is now giving out the sentence. "You will then return there after supper and clean the bathroom. If I find that you haven't properly cleaned the bathroom or that you have left the bunkhouse except for the evening program, you will be confined to the bunkhouse for all of tomorrow."

After a suitable pause in which he stared at them and they looked at the ground Mr. Williams continued, "Do you have any questions?"

Three heads silently moving left and right signified that there were no questions. Mr. Williams then added, "You boys are dismissed. Go back to the bunkhouse."

Once the boys were on their way Mr. Williams turned back towards me. "Well, Fruitgarden, you are once again in the middle of it," He commented. "Go get some dry clothes on and try to stay out of harms way for a while."

"I'll try," I answered back sincerely. "But it isn't easy."

Mr. Williams looked at me with a knowing smile and a nodding of his head in the affirmative. Then he pointed me in the direction of the bunkhouse and walked off to see what mischief the other boys might be up to.

As I walked gingerly towards Bunkhouse Two I was intercepted by a boy around my age who was riding a horse. He pulled in nice and close like he was driving a sports car and knew exactly what he was doing. He came right up to me so that I began to feel a little uneasy about being so close to a large horse. Looking down from his perch on top of the reddish brown horse he smiled and then spoke in a friendly voice, "You city boys might not know it, but around here we use swimming suits when we want to go in the water."

At first I thought he was making fun of me and I was about to make a fine retort about how country boys didn't know anything about anything. But as I looked into his eyes I could see that he was just making fun of life and the funny things that happen, he was not making fun of me. This at first surprised me and then after a moments reflection, pleased me.

So in the good nature that he had offered I responded with, "Well, I was just thinking that I didn't know what the customs were here and I didn't want to offend anyone."

He gave a genuine laugh as he absorbed my comment and in that moment we somehow knew that we were meeting another person that we were going to get along with just fine. He reached down towards me with his right hand and said, "My name is Ken, Ken Hutchins."

"Nice to meet you Ken," I replied reaching for his hand. "I'm Harry, Harry Fruitgarden."

As we shook hands and looked into each others eyes I again felt an instant kinship with Ken. I couldn't say why, but I just knew that here was a boy that I could just be me with, I wouldn't have to be worried about mind games and mean spirited teasing.

"Well, Harry, I have got some chores to finish up before dinner, so I'll see you later, " Ken said as he backed his horse away like a professional rodeo rider. "Better get some dry clothes on." He pointed at me, smiled and then turned his horse and galloped off like the lone ranger.

I was properly impressed with his horsemanship. I had never been so close to a full sized horse so I was also somewhat awed by the fact that he was in complete control of such a large animal. I had been on a pony ride at a small carnival once before. That had been fun, but not real horseback riding.

I had certainly fantasized about riding horses. There were any number of movie characters that rode horses. I loved western movies which were filled with all kinds of horses. I had read the books, *My Friend Flicka* and *Great Beauty*, but I had never spent any time with horses. Ken's obvious ability brought me down to earth and I realized that reading about horses wasn't the same as knowing how to ride them. I had a lot to learn.

Once back at the bunkhouse I changed into some fresh clothes. Fortunately Eric and his friends were in

Bunkhouse One, so I didn't have to be around them all of the time. But still, I would have to keep my eye out for them, they might want some revenge for the trouble I got them in. They wouldn't bother to consider that they were the ones that had caused the problem in the first place.

Knowing that I would be learning to ride horses I had brought some cowboy boots. It occurred to me that this was as good a time as any to break them in. I put on my boots and stood up to see how they looked. As I stood there next to my bed I flexed my knees in a simulated horseback riding position. Looking around to make sure I was alone, I then visualized holding the reins in my hands and as if I was trying to stop the horse I called out, "Whoa boy!", like I had seen in the movies. It felt pretty good.

No sooner had I stopped my imaginary horse then I heard a distant rumbling. Actually, I felt it coming through the concrete floor of the bunkhouse before I heard it. It felt and then sounded like the approach of a train, but I knew there were no train tracks in the area so it couldn't be that. For a moment, being that I am from California, I thought maybe there was an earthquake in the works. I had felt a couple of earthquakes before so I had some experience with them, this seemed different. I wasn't sure what was happening. I just knew that whatever it was, it was happening big.

Chapter 12

I decided to step outside to see if anyone else had noticed this strange occurrence. At first I saw nothing and no one. The rumbling in the ground and the sound that I couldn't quite place kept growing as I looked around. I saw a boy come running around the corner of Bunkhouse One with a look of terror on his face. He ran for all he was worth until he got to the door of the Bunkhouse One and then bounded through it to safety.

I had taken a couple of steps outside Bunkhouse Two, but now I instinctively stepped back into the shelter of the doorway. My eyes widened and my heart started to thump like the pounding that was coming through the earth. Then when the sound seemed to be almost on top of me I saw what was happening.

Around the corner of the lodge there appeared a herd of horses which soon came thundering towards the bunkhouses. They were running at a strong pace and the lead horse appeared to be filled with the thrill of being in front. It was a white horse with a streaming mane. The horse looked strong and spirited, his pounding hooves seemed to be a call of challenge to anyone who might oppose him and the power of the herd. Just before they arrived right in front of me the lead horse neighed for all he was worth. I was transfixed!

The next thing I knew was that they were all moving right past me between the bunkhouses. I was just eight or ten feet from the closest horses. They were in a tight pack and they seemed to run as one unit. Even though there were tall and short horses with slightly different strides, the horses seemed somehow to run in synchronicity with each other.

They caused a wind to blow by me with the strength of their forward progress. The overwhelming sound of their hoof-beats filled my head. I could smell the odor of grassy fields and dust as they went by. I was filled with the power and wonder of their presence, it was thrilling!

As the rear of the pack approached I could see their ranks were thinning. I figured maybe forty or fifty horses had run by. These were the stragglers, horses that for whatever reason didn't run with the main herd, I knew about that kind of position in my own life so I could feel for them.

A couple of them kicked up their heels as they went by. I got the impression that they too wanted to be a part of the show. They were feeling spunky, but not spunky enough to run in front.

Then I saw a horse and rider come streaking around the main lodge in pursuit of the herd. The rider was leaning forward and urging his horse to gain more speed. It seemed to me that he was going plenty fast already, I couldn't imagine him going faster. When the rider passed I saw that it was Ken Hutchins. I think it took some time for my jaw to raise up from its slack position - which exposed most of the inner part of my mouth.

Ken looked like an old time pony express rider that was trying to set a record between mail stops. His upper body was low and extended out in front of the saddle. His horse's mane was streaming up into his face but he didn't seem to mind. I could see his hands holding the reins loose so that the horse could extend its stride. It was exciting, thrilling, and amazing, all rolled up into one. My mind was leaping forward with the speed of the horses. When it landed I had a very clear thought: I want to do that!

I was so excited by what I saw that as they passed I ran out of the doorway and followed them past the bunkhouses. Once they were clear from the buildings they spread out and pranced through a large open meadow that separated the bunkhouses from the horse corrals. At the corral they merged into a four abreast file so that they could fit through a wide gate.

Some of the horses seemed unsure about going through the gate. I watched with admiration as Ken wove back and forth behind them, whooping with his voice and waving his hat to encourage the wayward horses to go through and join the herd on the other side of the fence.

Finally when all the horses were through Ken rode up to the gate and closed it without getting off his horse. Then he rode about forty feet to a small building with a hitching rail in front. There he unsaddled his horse and led it back to the gate. Once at the gate he opened it and released his horse on the other side. Free to join the herd, Ken's horse neighed as she approach the rest of the horses.

A few minutes later a truck came rumbling down the road with bales of hay in the back. When it passed through the gate it stopped on the other side and waited for Ken to climb up on the back. Fascinated by this whole process I ran from my position towards the corral. Once at the fence I stepped up onto the bottom rail so I could see what was happening. The truck was moving slowly as portions of hay were pushed out the back in little clumps. Soon all of the horses were all spread out with their long necks reaching down to little piles of hay.

While I watched the horses eat I noticed that not all of them wanted to share. Some of the smaller horses had to move from pile to pile so that they could steal a bite and move on. There was constant shuffling and maneuvering for position. One horse even tried - unsuccessfully - to control two piles. A couple of horses started kicking at each other which caused Ken to yell at them to stop - which they did, although I wasn't absolutely sure that Ken's yelling had caused them to stop. In any case, it appeared that Ken knew exactly what he was doing.

There were large horses, medium sized horses and even a pony. Some of the horses were black, others were brown and still others were pale yellow or white or speckled. Each horse seemed to have its own personality. I had never thought about horses having personalities. That made me wonder what I would look like if I were a horse.

When the truck was empty of hay it drove back towards the gate. I could see Ken in the back of the truck standing with his hands up on the cab. When they approached the gate he saw me and waved. Then he yelled out, "Hey Harry, will you get the gate for us?

Would I? Oh yes. I wanted to be part of this. Opening a gate looked like as good a spot as any to start.

I ran over to the gate, fumbled a little with the latch, but got it open in a reasonable length of time. As the truck rolled by Ken smiled at me. Then I closed the gate and walked over to the truck which had stopped in front of the shed. Ken and the driver of the truck were having a somewhat heated discussion.

"You are going to get it," The driver was saying.

"It wasn't my fault," Ken said in his own defense.

I had no idea what they were talking about, but I knew well the tones of voice and the need to defend ones position. I was instantly sympathetic to Ken's position.

"Well I doubt your Dad is going to see it that way," The driver continued. "But I guess we'll see."

Ken didn't respond to that. I could see by his face that he wasn't looking forward to it. When Ken noticed me hovering he decided to change the subject.

"Oh Harry, come meet my cousin Maurice." Ken said by way of introduction.

"Hi," I said looking at the driver of the truck. The driver didn't look too many years older than me. I wondered if he was really old enough to have a drivers license.

"Hi Harry," Maurice responded, stretching out his hand. "You just get in today?"

"Yes," I replied as I shook his hand.

"Well, welcome to Circle H Ranch." Maurice said with sincerity.

"Thanks," I said back.

Then Maurice looked down at my boots. "Looks like you got some new boots, you should get Ken to show you how to break them in."

I looked at Ken to see if he thought this was a good idea and apparently he did. "Sure, I'll help you out. But we need to do it in the morning around breakfast time."

I had no idea what breaking in boots and breakfast could have in common, but I agreed to meet Ken the next morning outside the kitchen door right after breakfast.

Then Maurice said, "I've got to get going. The dinner bell will be ringing soon. See you guys later." Maurice then drove off leaving Ken and I outside the shed.

I never knew if what happened next was a test or whether Ken just knew I wanted to participate in all that was going on. When Ken entered the shed and started straightening things up I just followed him in and started helping. I didn't know exactly what to call the things that I was straightening up, but there was an obvious logic to where things that looked the same should go. We worked for a few minutes in silence and then out of the blue Ken said, "This is the tack house." Tack is all the stuff you put on horses to ride them."

I nodded that I understood and then he started pointing at things. "That is a bridle," He said pointing at some pieces of leather and metal that I had seen on the head of the horse he had been riding.

"That is a saddle," I said pointing with a smile to a saddle that hung on the rail that stuck out from the wall.

Ken stopped what he was doing for a moment to look at me and see what my observation really meant. Was I being a smart aleck, had I been offended by his teaching me, or was I just sincerely entering into the learning process. He apparently realized that I was actually just enthusiastic about knowing something. So he went on. There are different kinds of saddles and bridles. I'll tell you about them as time goes on. We all ride western saddles here, not English style saddles, but there are still differences between western saddles."

Pointing at some different saddles on the wall he continued, "You see how some have low backs and some have high backs?"

"Yes, I see," I responded. "Why is that?"

"Well, partly it is like different shape chairs. People just feel comfortable in different shapes depending on the shape of their rear ends," He said with a chuckle. "But it also depends on what you are doing on the horse. Some are better for roping, some are better for staying on when a horse is bucking. And others are mostly for show."

I nodded my head up and down as I absorbed this information with interest.

"What kind do you use?" I asked.

Ken pointed to his saddle. Compared to the other saddles it appeared to have a middle-sized slope in the back and just enough bulk up front to lock your knees in if the horse started to buck. I determined that that was the kind of saddle that I would want to use.

"I'll show you some more stuff tomorrow," Ken said. "The supper bell is going to ring soon and we need to wash up first."

Soon we had closed up the tack house and were walking back towards the lodge.

As we walked back Ken asked, "Have you ever ridden a horse, Harry?"

"Not really," I answered truthfully. "I was on a little pony ride once, but I don't think that counts."

"Well, tomorrow we will get you up on a horse and you can see if you like it," Ken said.

"Oh, I know I'm going to like it," I responded. "I'm just not sure how good I will be at staying on, to say nothing of steering."

Ken stopped for a moment and looked at me with an appraising eye. I got the feeling that he was checking me out the way he might look at a horse to see if it was worth riding. After a while he gave me a nod and a grin. "I think you will be all right Harry Fruitgarden," Ken said confidently.

The supper bell caught his attention as he was looking at me. "Oh boy, I'm going to be late and I'm already in trouble," announced Ken. Before I could ask him why he was in trouble he turned towards the main lodge and started to run. Calling back over his shoulder he said, "I'll see you later." And then he ran like trouble was close on his heels.

Once again, I could feel inside that Ken was my kind of guy. I felt like I had made a new friend that I had always known; it was strange, warm and kind of nice. Camp in Colorado was looking pretty good right now. But the day wasn't yet over, there were still some ups and downs to ride before I could get some rest.

Chapter 13

I made my way back to the bunkhouse, washed up and followed along with some of the other boys who were heading to the lodge for dinner. At the lodge we found a side entrance that went directly into the dining room. Stepping inside we were bathed in the sounds of animated talking, silverware clinking on plates and the odors of a home cooked meal.

There were several rows of long tables that had red and white checkerboard table cloths. In the back of the room was a kitchen that you could see into through the buffet style service area. There were ten or twelve boys waiting to be served so I took my place at the back of the line.

As I stood in line I noticed that diners were shoveling the food in with gusto. I guessed that meant it tasted good, which I took as a good omen because I was pretty hungry and I didn't have much in the way of back-up food in the bunkhouse for emergencies. Just the smell of food made my mouth start to water. As I moved forward in the line my stomach and eager taste buds began to send excited messages of anticipation to my brain.

By the time it was my turn to grab a plate and eating utensils at the front of the serving line I was so focused on eating that I hardly noticed anything else. The women serving the food ladled it on as we passed in front of them. They were friendly and kept a constant "Welcome to Circle H Ranch!" going as boys passed by with plates that became heavy with food.

The first woman offered some kind of casserole. I handled that with one hand holding my plate, but it did dip a bit when the food landed. The second lady gave me a good portion of mashed potatoes. That caused me to send my left hand up to help my right hand steady the plate. The gravy didn't cause much of a problem after that, nor did the vegetables that were added to almost fill the plate.

The ladies voices were very sincere and friendly but I have to admit that I was more focused on the food than their greetings; I hardly looked up at them. The aromas that were steaming their way up towards my nose had my full attention. My plate was heavily laden with food and my arms were extended to hold the plate near them. I was just about to pull my plate back when I was struck dumb by an unexpected event.

Yes, I would have to call this an event - not just something that happened, but a real, genuine event.

As I stood there beginning to withdraw my plate from further bounty a voice broke through my awareness of muscle fatigue and good smells to penetrate to the roots of my being. "Oh, don't you want some rolls?" A friendly voice that I had not yet registered with a face asked.

That voice alone was sufficient to shock my system to complete attention. Why that should have been so I couldn't even begin to say until I looked up. As my eyes moved from the mound of potatoes on my plate to a face that was even more beautiful than the voice, I was struck with a complete ecstatic paralysis. My mind and body just locked up as if a switch had been flipped somewhere in my brain. I just stood there staring at this angelic face that had a beautiful voice.

Somewhere deep in the back of my mind there was a momentary flash of understanding. This is a beautiful girl. Be cool. Act cool. And don't under any circumstances make a fool of yourself.

Unfortunately that little mental spark was just a fantasy. I was instantaneously in over my head and I knew it. I struggled mightily inside myself to animate my body and mind but it was like all of the connections to thought and motion had been severed. I had to say something, but nothing was forthcoming. I stood there motionless for so long that she must have assumed that I was hard of hearing. So she looked at me, extended the rolls, and twitched her eyes in a way that said: Do you want some?

That little twitch of her eyebrows was devastating. Any chance of recovery was now completely gone. I was mentally mush. My heart was thumping. My palms were starting to sweat. I desperately needed help because I couldn't help myself. Fortunately an impatient fellow behind me in line saved me from total and complete disaster.

"Hey, Fruitgarden!" He called out with irritation while simultaneously bumping me in the side. "Get moving. We're hungry back here."

I could have hugged him for helping me out – even though he didn't know he was doing so. His agitation and bump got my internal system up and running. It was kind of like when you bump a machine to get it to cooperate. Anyway, it worked sufficiently to get me moving again.

I still couldn't speak, but I was able to extend my plate for a roll and turn the corners of my mouth up into a smile. When she smiled back as she placed the roll on my plate I almost lost it again. I noticed that her eyes were blue, they were really clear and deep. I began to look into her eyes and started to lose control again when I was grabbed firmly by the shoulder and ushered towards the tables.

"Mr. Fruitgarden," Began the voice of Mr. Williams as he pushed me forward. "I don't know what you are up to, but whatever it is it will have to wait until after dinner, you're holding up the line."

I grinned all the way to a seat at the very end of the last row of tables. I sat quietly eating my food and between bites I grinned. I hardly noticed the taste of the food. I mentally reviewed what had just happened, playing it over and over again in my head. I determined that no matter how foolish I had appeared, it was worth it just so I could look into those incredible eyes.

By the time that I had recovered sufficiently to look back at the serving counter the line was empty and the angelic face was gone. I figured that was just as well because my nervous system was still in shock, it would take some time to recover. And besides, the mental picture of her face was etched into my mind so clearly that I could now gaze inwardly at my leisure to absorb her presence without fear of making a fool of myself.

When I was midway through my plate of food an announcement was made that an evening program would begin at 7:30 p.m. Since it was only about 6 p.m. now I figured I would take my time eating. Most of the room was empty when I took my dirty dishes up to the counter. There I found a bucket into which I could scrape off any items not eaten and two deep trays partially filled with water for plates and silverware. I looked around one last time for the beautiful face, but she was not to be seen.

Next to the dining room I found the main hall of the lodge. It was a large room with a big open fireplace. There was a large semicircular step in front of the fireplace and then chairs and couches had been laid out for a good-sized group to face the fire. On the side of the room towards the front was a large upright piano. To the left of the fireplace there was a very large box into which piles of firewood had been thrown. The ceiling had huge pine poles as rafters and the walls were wood as well. It had a warm friendly feeling.

There were double doors on both sides of the room, which led to private rooms. I guessed that this is where some of the adults stayed. The only other door was the main entrance, which led to a covered deck that ran along the front of the lodge

I walked out the front and looked around at the colorful sky, pine trees and river. It was really beautiful. The air was cooling with day's end. High in the sky long thin clouds were bathed in red and orange colors. There was the scent of pine and grass floating by on a light breeze. The river made pleasant noises as it flowed peacefully by, the earth was radiant and alive.

Boys were swarming on the bridge. A couple of boys had their fishing poles extended over the side in hopes of an end of the day catch. I decided to walk in the opposite direction around the corner of the lodge, I hadn't been to this part of camp yet. I soon found several small cabins. I didn't walk too close to them because I didn't want to disturb anyone and I didn't want people to think I was snooping around.

I found a pigpen under some pine trees and leaned over the rail to watch several large pigs and some piglets. I thought the pigs were kind of cute, but they were also mighty smelly – and I don't mean in a good way - so I moved on and found a small building with several old fashioned washing machines. I gathered from the sheets on the clotheslines that the equipment was still service-able.

Just as I was rounding a corner towards the back of the kitchen I came upon a man and a boy talking. Well, not exactly talking. The man was chewing out the boy pretty well.

I didn't mean to eavesdrop, but I couldn't help hearing the man say sternly, "I can't believe you did that. With all of these new boys in camp someone could have gotten hurt. I have to be able to count on your good judgement."

By the time I realized what was happening I had rounded the corner and it was too late to retreat. Fortunately they saw me right away and the man stopped his lecture. Then I noticed immediately that Ken Hutchins was the one that was in trouble. Now I knew what Maurice had been referring to when we were back at the tack house.

I didn't know the details of the situation, but I knew the general theme. I had been called out on the carpet many times by my Dad so I was very experienced in situations like this. I decided to see what I could do to help Ken out.

"Excuse me," I said. "I didn't mean to interrupt you. I was just looking around to see the place."

Ken didn't hesitate to take advantage of this for-tuitous opportunity to change the subject.

"Dad," Ken said with enthusiasm. "This is Harry Fruitgarden. He just arrived today."

Ken's father put on a smile right away and stepped towards me extending has hand. "Hi Harry," He said. "I am Dan Hutchins."

I stepped forward and immediately felt embraced by Mr. Hutchins' friendliness. He looked me right in the eyes and gave me a sincere smile.

"Nice to meet you, Mr. Hutchins," I said shaking his hand. "This sure is a beautiful place."

I figured Mr. Hutchins would say something like: Well, Thank You. Then I expected that like most people, he would puff up a bit with the compliment; but he didn't. He calmly looked around at the mountains and trees with a smile on his face. Mr. Hutchins kept a hold of my hand while he seemed to mentally absorb the moment. "Yes," Mr. Hutchins then said with a kind of contentment. "It truly is beautiful."

It was like he totally entered into the truth of the statement, not because I said it, but because it was true. Then he looked at me to see if I really believed it. When he saw that I did, he smiled again and let go of my hand.

I knew right away that this was a man that I could be straight with, and that he would be straight with me. I was starting to feel like I was meeting a whole family of people that I could feel at home with.

Then without skipping a beat Mr. Hutchins said, "Why don't you boys go feed the pigs?"

Chapter 14

Ken answered his father with a "Yes Sir!" so fast that I hardly had a chance to keep up with him as he turned around and headed for the back door of the kitchen. I knew well the signs of someone who has narrowly escaped disaster and is heading with all speed in the opposite direction.

As we entered the kitchen I turned back and said to Mr. Hutchins, "Nice to meet you, Sir."

Mr. Hutchins smiled and nodded his head. I could see that he knew what was happening with his son's escape. I sensed that he was relieved as well, I don't think he liked being angry at his son. That made me pause to think that Ken was a lucky boy indeed: Horses and a kindhearted father, that was not a bad combination.

Once we were in the kitchen and out of earshot of his father Ken turned to me and said, "Thanks, Harry. You saved me from some trouble there."

"No problem, "I replied. "I have been there many times myself. So, what exactly were you in trouble for?"

"Well," Ken said. "When I went out to get the horses back to the corral this afternoon I was riding a horse that gets spooked easily."

"Whoa," I interjected, already being infected by cowboy talk. "What does it mean when a horse gets spooked?"

"It is just like with people on Halloween," Ken said. "Except for some horses everyday is Halloween and the least little thing is spooky to them. It can be a smell they don't like, unexpected movement, sounds or pretty much anything that they just don't like. When they get spooked they can jump around, try to run off, and sometimes even start to buck."

"Okay, so what happened this afternoon?" I asked encouraging him to continue his story.

"I rode out to the far meadow to the get the horses from where they were grazing," Ken continued. "Usually I just get behind them all and with a little whooping they start off towards the corral nice and slow. They know it is feeding time, so it isn't like they don't want to go. Well, we got about halfway back and my horse stepped on a piece of wood that made a loud cracking sound that he didn't like. The next thing I know he's bumping into a horse next to us. Then that horse bumped into another and there was a chain reaction. That caused all of the horses to get excited and start running for all they were worth. By the time I got my horse calmed down and the gate to the meadow shut the whole herd had bolted for home."

His story explained perfectly why the horses had come running through camp. I could understand his situation and how it had not been his fault, at the same time, I could also understand his father's concern for the safety of the campers. It felt slightly odd to me to see both points of view, I could see how in some ways they were both in the right. I was also impressed that Ken had been given such a big responsibility at his age, my Dad wouldn't have trusted me with anything like that.

I wasn't sure if I was supposed to say something in support of Ken but I was saved from comment when he said, "Now that my father has told me how he feels it will be over. Next time I will be double careful about not starting a stampede."

Signaling that this story was over, Ken walked over to four buckets of table scraps from the day's meals. We each grabbed two buckets and headed out towards the pigpen. The buckets were pretty heavy and the odor was quite ripe. The contents sloshed around as we walked so I tried to hold the buckets out from my sides to avoid being splashed. It wasn't easy, but I didn't complain. I just did my best and walked as fast as I could.

When we arrived at the pigpen the pigs seemed to know what was up and began to snort up a storm. They stood up from their muddy bed and began to prance around with enthusiasm. The little piglets scattered so as not to be trampled by the bigger pigs. Those little guys were pretty cute even if they were stinky.

I took Ken's lead and tipped my bucket over the edge of the fence into a long trough. As I poured out the odorous contents I had to try and stand back to avoid being splashed. Ken saw me twitch a little as I tried to stay out of the way and he started to laugh. Then after a momentary pause, so did I because I realized that Ken was laughing with me, not at me. He wasn't putting me down; he was just enjoying the humor of the moment. Now I knew why they called the food in these buckets pig slop, it was for the pigs and it was really sloppy!

When the buckets were empty we watched the pigs nose around in their food. Apparently they were very happy with the menu. They gobbled up the food with gurgling and grunting sounds that seemed to say, "Pretty fine grub!"

Once back at the kitchen we rinsed out the buckets with water and placed them back where they could be used again tomorrow. As we headed out of the kitchen Ken turned to me and said, "Be sure to meet me here right after breakfast and we will take care of your boots."

I still wasn't sure what the kitchen and my boots had to do with each other, but I agreed to meet him after breakfast. Then Ken seemed to pause for a second, I could see that he was thinking about something. When Ken was done turning the cogs in his mind he asked me, "Harry, tonight at the program there will be some skits. When a new group arrives we like to choose someone to join the Loyal Order of the Chicken. Would you be interested in being initiated into this special group?"

Well I wasn't used to being invited to join special groups. I figured if Ken was in it, I wanted to be in it. So without asking any questions I said, "Sure, sounds good to me."

"Okay," Ken said. "When we get up for the initiation just follow my lead. You will be fine. I have to make some preparations for the ceremony so I'll see you there. Thanks again for helping me out with my father and feeding the pigs." Before I could respond Ken was running off once again. This time it was into the darkening sky as sunset turned to evening.

I decided to head for the bunkhouse to get my flashlight before it got fully dark. Then with flashlight in hand I made my way back to the main lodge. I couldn't help wondering what I had gotten myself into. My instinct was to trust Ken, but the *Loyal Order of the Chicken* sounded pretty strange. I had no idea what it was all about. In the back of my mind little red flags were trying to twitch.

When I arrived at the Lodge people were already gathering. There were just a few campers besides our group. As the lodge filled I noticed a number of adults that I hadn't seen before. I looked for the angelic face from the dinner counter but didn't see any young girls around. I sat on the side towards the back. As I looked around I felt a little strange. Even though I had arrived with thirty-nine other boys, I felt like I was alone here at camp. No that wasn't exactly right. In some strange way I felt like I was at home and all these boys were visitors.

The fireplace had a roaring fire in it and soon the room was filled with loud voices telling tall tales of the day's adventures. I heard one boy mention that he had almost gotten caught by the stampede. Another boy was showing with his hands the size of a fish that got away. At one point I caught Eric Winston glaring at me. I gave him a quick wink and moved on. Apparently he wasn't going to forget the trouble that he had gotten himself into that he now considered my fault. I would have to keep an eye out for his attempt at revenge.

The raucous sounds of the group were brought to an end when someone began to play the piano. The song sounded like a tune from an old cowboy movie, it was perfect for setting the scene in an old western. The man playing the piano was very good and when he was done he stood up to a hearty round of applause.

Once the clapping had abated he introduced himself. "Greetings," He said in a warm and friendly voice. "For those of you who have just arrived, welcome to the Circle H Ranch. We're glad that you are all here and that you arrived safely. My name is Andrew Jonas, but most people call me Jonesy. I will be your master of ceremonies at these evening powwows. Just so you know, none of us are professional entertainers, but I expect we will have some fun."

He then went on to introduce Mr. Hutchins and Mrs. Hutchins as the owners of the camp. He also introduced his own wife and several other adults that help to run the camp. He invited everyone to help at future evening programs by coming up with skits.

"Now… ladies and gentlemen," He said in a classic ring announcer's voice, "direct from the Grand Ole Opry…on special engagement here at Circle H Ranch…I present to you…the Hutchins Sisters."

Then Jonesy ran to the piano and started to play up a storm of introduction music. Out from behind the door to the dinning hall came four girls dressed like poor country girls with pigtails and red rouge on their cheeks. They looked like cartoon characters. They all had big grins on their faces and one of the girls had a tooth that they had blackened so that it looked like she was missing it. They looked very funny and everyone started to laugh and clap.

For their first number they sang the classic campfire song, Clementine. Once they got things going everyone joined in on the chorus. One of the girls even had shoebox shoes. They really hammed it up. I was laughing my head off. None of us seemed to notice that it was really a very sad song.

These four girls were apparently the daughters of Mr. and Mrs. Hutchins. It was a little hard to tell what they would look like without their makeup and costumes, but they all seemed to be unselfconscious and willing to have a good time. I could easily tell this wasn't their first performance. This type of entertainment was apparently part of the family's lifestyle.

They knew all of the verses of Clementine – most of which I had never heard – and when they were done there was thunderous applause. There was even some whooping and whistling. When the tumult receded they began a second song, *After The Ball Was Over*. I had never heard this song. It was about an old woman that had more to take off than most at the end of the day. Along with her gown she had to remove a fake eye, false teeth and a peg leg. Each new part that had to be removed caused the audience to laugh harder. It was downright sad and hilarious at the same time.

It was during the next and final song that I observed something that I hadn't noticed before. The girls were lined up from tallest on the left to shortest on the right. I took this to be an indication of their ages as well. The girl on the far left looked to be about nineteen or twenty. The next, I would guess, was about seventeen. The third seemed maybe fifteen and the last around my age: twelve.

It was the last girl that really caught my eye. During the first two songs I had been so taken up with the overall affect of their costumes and singing that I hadn't looked closely at their faces. When I took the time to look carefully I recognized the eyes of the last girl. They were the same blue eyes that had affected me so strongly in the food line. I didn't hear much of the song after that, I don't even remember what the name of the song was; I just stared at her.

When the song ended and the applause started I twitched up to my feet for a standing ovation before I could think what I was doing. The next thing I knew everyone was looking at me instead of the girls up front. I looked around in panic not knowing what to do and then looked back to find her looking right at me. Once again I was struck dumb and stopped clapping with my hands in front of me just sticking out in the air. I was standing there like a creature frozen in time through some quirk of nature. But I didn't care because she was looking right at me.

Chapter 15

As I stood there taking in a kind of magic feeling there was a part of me that could tell that I was attracting undue attention to myself. The really strange thing was that I didn't care; it was like I was mesmerized.

There is no way of saying how long I would have stood there on my own. Fortunately we will never know, because I was saved by their parents. They apparently felt that a standing ovation was a good idea. Once Mr. and Mrs. Hutchins had stood up, the whole crowd was on their feet. Apparently this was a first at Circle H Ranch. That caused the girls to be slightly embarrassed and they all started to giggle and run off towards the door.

I probably would have been okay to sit down after that except that a most wondrous thing happened. Just as the girls were about to exit they turned back and looked at the audience while they waved goodbye. This seemed to be a part of their performance because as they did it Jonesy stood up and introduced the girls by name.

"Let's give a final round of applause to Kathy, Wendy, Sarah and Shannon," Jonesy barked out with accents on each name.

Just as he said Shannon, the last girl looked me right in the eyes and winked. Ahhh....that was a great moment.

Then they were gone and everyone was sitting down as the applause tapered off. In a daze I too sat down, but not for long. I didn't even have time to contemplate the many possible meanings of that heavenly wink.

"Once again, ladies and gentlemen, we have a special moment to share with you," Jonesy began.

I had no idea what was coming next but Jonesy's style was captivating.

"We are now about to witness a seldom seen event," announced Jonesy. "Normally this special ceremony is held in secret. But tonight we are being given the special opportunity to observe an ancient ritual. To explain let me introduce the Grand Chicken of the Loyal Order of Chickens, Mr. Ken Hutchins."

There was a hearty applause as Ken stepped from behind the dinning room door to take the stage. He was followed by two other boys around the same age who were holding folding chairs that they placed side by side in a row behind Ken.

Ken started things off with an introduction, "Ladies and gentlemen, I am Ken Hutchins, Grand Chicken of the Loyal Order of Chickens." He said this with such a solemn voice that there were surprisingly few chuckles. To those who let laughter squeak out of their mouths he gave a suitably dignified glare. It was clear from his demeanor that this was to be a serious occasion even though the name of the group, Loyal Order of Chickens, was in itself pretty funny.

Ken continued, "This evening we will be initiating a new member into our order. We normally do not share this special time with outsiders."

At the use of the word outsiders he swept the audience with his eyes. He was saying very clearly that we had better behave ourselves. The few laughs that were let loose uncontrollably were quickly squelched.

"My brother chickens and I now call up the honored candidate," Ken announced. "Will Mr. Harry Fruitgarden please step forward."

His announcement took me by surprise, even though we had discussed it earlier. I was so caught up with trying to think about Shannon that I had forgotten I would be participating in this ceremony.

There were a few polite applause as I stood up and made my way forward. I could hear some whispering floating around the room, but I couldn't tell what was being said. I began to think that this wasn't such a good idea, but it was too late to do anything about it.

Ken greeted me with a firm handshake. Then he spoke for all to hear, "As we welcome Mr. Fruitgarden to our sacred order we must insist on silence during the ceremony. There most be absolutely no laughing. This is a very solemn occasion."

Of course that caused a few boys to laugh. Once again he swept the room with glaring eyes that tried to say that no exceptions were to be made. When the room was once again quiet the ceremony proceeded.

I was led to the last of four chairs. As I sat down the boy who sat next to me, whom I had not met before, whispered in my ear, "Just do what we do."

That seemed simple enough to me, so I just listened and watched.

Ken stood in front of his chair while the other boys sat in theirs. He announced that the ceremony was now going to begin and that silence should be observed.

Then after sitting in his chair so long that it seemed that nothing would happen he jumped up suddenly and yelled, "I am a dog!" Ken then started to bark loud and strong.

The audience tried to stay quiet but laughter was inevitable. When the next boy jumped up and made the same pronouncement the audience stayed pretty quiet, but when he started to yap like a little lap dog they lost it with laughter.

Ken immediately stood up and berated the audience for their lack of control. Once quiet was again achieved the third boy jumped up and made his pronouncement. He too was a dog and when he barked the audience once again laughed.

When it became my turn I decided that I should enter fully into the moment. Jumping up with enthusiasm I proclaimed, "I am a dog." As I gave what I considered to be a fairly realistic bark the audience began to clap. Then with a smile I sat down thinking that things were going to be just fine.

After the room had calmed down Ken jumped up with a new pronouncement, "I am a horse!" He then gave a hearty neigh.

By now it was clear what the format of the initiation would be. We each stood up in turn going through various farm animals. We continued through horse, cow, and pig. Finally we arrived at chicken. By now there was no pretense of quiet in the room. Each successive animal impression would bring new paroxysms of laughter to the group. Soon I was fully into performance mode. Anticipating that the chicken would be the last animal on the list I gave a thundering rooster impression. I took my time savoring the laughter and applause after my full-throated impression. I took a deep bow and as I slowly sat down I looked over at the other members of the Loyal Order of the Chicken to see what was next.

My fellow members were looking at me and starting to laugh. The fact that they were starting to laugh struck me as odd. They were no longer holding themselves upright and serious as before. It was like an item out of place in a room that you know well. My mind registered that there was something odd here, but I couldn't fathom what it might be.

Then as I sat on the chair my mind went into slow motion. I felt a lump in the chair as I sat, but it was too late to stop. Then there was a cracking/popping sound followed by a wet sticky sensation that came through my pants. I instantly knew there was a problem.

Just then Ken jumped up and announced to all, "Mr. Fruitgarden is now a member of the Loyal Order of Chicken and he has laid and broken his first egg!"

Now, as I automatically jumped up out of my seat, everyone knew why. I had just sat on and broken an egg. There was tremendous laughter and applause.

As I tried to look at my wet pants and then around the room, I noticed that some of the boys I had come with on the bus were laughing derisively at me while others were laughing in good fun. When I looked at Ken, who had masterminded this little episode, he walked up to me with a friendly smile and patted me on the shoulder while saying, "Welcome to the club!"

In that moment I knew that if I took this in the right spirit I truly would be "In the Club". I smiled at him and laughed without rancor. It really was a pretty good gag. We then went into the kitchen and I wiped off my pants as best I could.

The rest of the evening was filled with group singing, followed by a few announcements about tomorrow's plans. After breakfast in the morning there would be horseback riding, which would be followed in the afternoon by fishing.

The last song of the evening was the old standard, Kumbya. As we all sang the room became calm and quiet. Then after the song someone led a prayer thanking God for our safe arrival at camp and expressing appreciation for all the bounty in our lives. At the end of the prayer some people said, "In the name of Jesus Christ, Amen."

I knew that there were quite a few boys from Jewish families in our group. I wondered what they thought about this, and I wondered if our parents knew that this would be part of our experience. I didn't know much about Jesus, but I did know that the ideas expressed by the prayer were good ideas, so I took that as a reason to feel good about the prayers being said.

The evening was then over and everyone started to head back to the bunkhouses. Ken came up behind me and reminded me to meet him behind the kitchen after breakfast. Then I headed out to into the night.

Outside, flashlight beams were bobbing through the night like fireflies. Boys were walking in small groups while they recapped the activities of the evening. When I arrived at the bunkhouse most of the bunks were filled with boys that looked like they were ready to embrace a good night's sleep. I brushed my teeth and got into my sleeping bag.

It didn't take too long for the lights to go out. Lying on my bed I found that my mind was racing with thoughts from my day's activities. We had started this day in Mesa Verde with the mummy incident and then the cliff dwellings. That had been followed by our arrival at camp. Since that time I had been dunked in the river, there had been a stampede, I met Ken and his father, I started to learn about horses, I helped feed the pigs, I had been initiated into the Loyal Order of the Chicken, and I had met Shannon. I could hardly believe this had only been one day and I had only been here at camp for a few hours. It seemed like a much longer time than that. If every day at camp was going to be like today I was going to be mighty exhausted!

As my mind wandered from one exciting moment to another I arrived back at thoughts of Shannon. There was something special there. I didn't know quite what it was, but I couldn't help what I was feeling – even though I didn't know exactly what those feelings meant!

I wished I could consult my brother Frank; he is a real ladies man. He knows how to talk to girls. It isn't that I am totally without experience with girls, I had learned to dance at the YMCA. I am pretty good at it and have danced at one time or another with most of the girls in my class. But that's not the same as having a private conversation. It also didn't seem to be of much value when I lost my head while just looking at Shannon. I was like a deer in the headlights. It was both frightening and wonderful at the same time. What was a guy supposed to do?

I decided that I would just have to wait and see how things progressed in that regard. In the meantime I would focus on horses. Tomorrow I would learn to ride a horse. I set my mind on the power and beauty of the horses as they came running through camp earlier in the day.

As slumber took me I found myself mentally riding a tall horse that was a dark color that seemed to shimmer. It was thrilling to see the world from the strength of her back. My last conscious impression before dipping fully into sleep was the feeling that I was somehow flying.

Chapter 16

I slept very soundly that night. There were no strange dreams and I had no feelings of being in a foreign new place. I was used to feeling a kind of restlessness that made me think that I was supposed to be in some better place if I could just figure out where that place might be; I didn't feel that here. My inner sense of well-being told me that I was now where I was supposed to be.

My mind rose from sleep of its own accord without registering any sounds or feelings of alarm. I just suddenly found that I was awake and rested. I looked out one of the windows that were placed high on the wall of the bunkhouse; it was light outside, but just barely.

I rose quietly, all of the other boys were sleeping; a few were snoring. One boy farted loudly as I walked down the aisle towards the bathroom - that made me walk a little faster. I decided that I would take a shower, brush my teeth and get outside.

It was a fine plan and I took it as a good sign that it went off without any major hitches. By the time I got outside the sky was light. The air was brisk so I wore my jacket. My new boots were a bit stiff, but they felt good. I have very narrow feet and most shoes don't snug up against the sides of my feet very well, these cowboy boots did feel snug without being too tight. My feet liked that.

I didn't have to think twice about where I was going, I headed straight for the corral, I wanted to watch the horses. When I got to the wooden rail fence I climbed up to the top and sat with my legs on the next rail down. The wood was just wide enough that it didn't dig too badly into my rear end.

The first thing that I noticed about the horses is that they were all staying fairly close together. They weren't all shoulder to shoulder, but only a few were more than ten or twelve feet from the next horse. The corral was pretty large, but the horses didn't seem to care. It struck me that this was a herd; they were staying close for protection. That thought led me to wondering if there was something that they needed protection from. We were definitely out in the wilderness; there might be bears or mountain lions. I looked all around but didn't see anything and then I laughed at myself for getting spooked.

It seemed like I could see horses of almost every color that a horse could be and each seemed to have its own look and personality. I counted over fifty horses. It was a little hard to tell because they moved around and I wasn't sure if I had counted some horses twice and some not at all. As I looked at the horses I began to wonder if it was possible to tell by looking at a horse what kind of horse it would be?

Then I wondered: What qualities would make a good horse? It would certainly need to be fast. But after that I wasn't sure. Quick turning seemed like a good ability. Jumping might be useful. Not easily spooked would also be nice based on what happened to Ken yesterday.

As I went through these ideas I noticed the horses start to get aroused. The whole group of them started to pick up their heads and look around. Hoofs began to paw at the ground and a general shuffling took place. I looked around but didn't see anything. Then I heard a truck approach from behind me. I turned to look and saw that it was the hay truck, the horses had known it was coming before I did. I jumped down and went over to open the gate.

Maurice was once again at the wheel and Ken was up top on the back, they smiled when they saw me. I opened the gate when the truck was close and was surprised to find that the truck stopped just on the other side.

Then Ken called down to me, "You gonna help or not?"

I didn't have to be asked twice. I closed the gate and jumped up on the back of the truck. Right away the truck started to move out towards the horses. Some of the horses moved right in behind the truck and tried to bite at the hay before it had even hit the ground. Ken showed me how much to push out at a time. He threw the hay out on the driver's side while I threw it out on the passenger's side. Maurice kept the truck moving at a slow but steady pace.

It took us about ten minutes to throw out all the hay. Some of the horses began to fight over little piles and Ken would yell at them to stop. Watching the horses kick at each other made me a little nervous. The idea of being the recipient of a kick like that was kind of scary.

As if he could read my mind Ken said without being asked, "Don't put yourself where you can get kicked and you won't get kicked. And always let a horse know you are there before you walk up behind him. If you don't…well you can't blame the horse if you spook him. Most horses only kick when they are mad or scared."

That made a lot of sense to me. I just didn't know how you could be around horses and never be near the rear end. But the question I asked was, "How do you know when they are upset by something?"

"Watch their ears," Ken replied. "The ears tell the whole story. Pointing front is happy and content. To the side is wondering if there is a problem. Laid back is I'm getting ready to do something you won't like."

I decided right then and there that I would have to become an expert at watching the ears of horses. Then I asked, "What do you do when you have to go around the back of a horse?"

Ken looked at me before answering. He seemed to approve of the question. He answered, "Well, you put your hand on his rump and you keep it between you and the horse as you go around. This does several things. It lets the horse know that you are the one going around the back. It also allows you to monitor the muscles of the horse. If you feel them tensing up or starting to move, you can get out of the way. It also acts as a kind of eject lever. If the horse starts to kick, by stiffening your arm you will be pushed away, hopefully before you get kicked. In any case, it will lessen the power of the kick if the horse does get you."

"Have you been kicked?" I asked Ken.

"Sure," He replied. "But it has been a while. Mostly it happens now when I get bucked off a horse and they kick you on your way down. Most horses won't kick you on purpose, although there are some that are just plain ornery. So you have to be careful, but I wouldn't worry about it."

I had never heard the word ornery before, but I got the meaning by just hearing the way Ken used it in a sentence. I hoped that I wouldn't be meeting any ornery horses too soon.

When we got to the gate I jumped down and did my opening and closing gate thing. Then I jumped back up on the truck and we headed towards the lodge. Ken and Maurice headed for the dining hall. I figured that it was too early to eat so I started to stay back. When Ken noticed I had stopped he turned towards me and said, "Its okay, wranglers can eat just as soon as the food is ready. We will need to be saddling up the horses while the others are getting their breakfast."

I wasn't exactly sure what a wrangler was. I guessed it was someone who worked with the horses. Ken seemed to think I was included in this group, so who was I to disagree? I walked in behind him and Maurice. When we walked up to the counter and started helping ourselves to food no one even looked at us. I noticed that Mrs. Hutchins was helping to cook. There was also another middle-aged woman helping. I didn't see Shannon, although I took care to look.

We loaded up with eggs and pancakes. I passed on the bacon but the others piled it on their plates like it was candy. We got some milk and sat down to eat. Maurice and Ken prayed silently before eating. I didn't pray, but I did sit quietly until they were done. Then, finding that I was really hungry, I dug in.

One thing that I was learning about the Circle H Ranch was that the food was good and that there was lots of it. I smiled while I ate.

Once we were done with breakfast Maurice took off for parts unknown while Ken and I walked right into the kitchen. I started to hesitate since I wouldn't think of doing this at school while cooks were on the job. But then I figured that Ken would let me know if there was a problem, so I went right in behind him.

121

Ken walked up to his mother and introduced me. "Mom," he said. "This is Harry Fruitgarden."

Since she was busy flipping pancakes she couldn't shake my hand, but Mrs. Hutchins turned towards me and smiled broadly. "Yes," She said with a chuckle. "You are the new member of the Loyal Order of Chicken aren't you?"

I nodded that she was correct, "Yes, I guess I am."

"Well, it is nice to meet you," She then said, deftly flipping another pancake.

"Mom, we were going to grease Harry's new boots," Ken said to his mother. "Is that okay?"

"Sure," She said. "Were done cooking the bacon. And besides, we can't have a new member of the Order getting his feet wet!" Then she turned back to her cooking with a chuckle.

I liked Mrs. Hutchins right away. She was friendly and had a broad embracing smile. She seemed like a person that was quick to hug and slow to scold.

I was beginning to get the impression that these were all people who assumed you were a good person until proven otherwise. I was used to being around people who expected you to prove yourself first before being accepted. I very much liked this inclusive approach to life.

Ken grabbed a hot pad and then a large pan of hot bacon grease. Heading for the door he said, "Harry, can you get the door?"

I jumped in front of him and pushed the door out as he came through behind me. Once we were outside he put the pan on the ground. Apparently it was pretty heavy.

"Okay Harry," He directed. "Take your boots off.

I wasn't sure what was about to take place but I was learning to trust Ken – even if he did arrange to have an egg slipped under me last night at the evening program.

Once my boots were off Ken started to pour the bacon grease on them. As he maneuvered the pan around to aim the grease he explained. "This bacon grease will waterproof your boots," He said. "It also softens them up when they are new, so you won't be as likely to get blisters."

I had never heard of this being done though it did make sense. The hot grease would penetrate into the leather and then leave a fatty coating to repel water.

"Just do this once in a while and your boots will stay dry in the rain or tall wet grass," He said, adding to my quickly growing store of horseman's knowledge.

After the grease had cooled I put my boots back on. They looked like they had aged a year and they smelled like bacon, but what the heck, they looked like they were ready to do their job.

Suddenly a question came to me so I asked Ken, "Why do cowboys wear these boots?"

Ken looked at me for a moment to see if I was serious. Finding that I was quite serious he burst out laughing. Then when he got done laughing he told me to come along and he would show me why cowboys wear boots.

Chapter 17

While Ken and I headed for the corral we passed most of the campers on their way to the dining hall to eat breakfast. Arriving at the tack house we found that Maurice already had three horses saddled and tied up to the long corral fence. We also found another fellow just arriving with three more horses ready to be saddled.

The boy arriving with the horses had been in the Loyal Order of the Chicken skit but we had never been officially introduced. When he saw me he smiled. Once he had tied the horses to the rail in front of the tack house he walked over and introduced himself.

"Hi, Harry," he said as he reached out to shake my hand. "I'm Andrew, but most people call me Andy. Maurice is my brother."

As I shook his hand I could tell that he was a genuinely friendly person. He was about my height and looked to be around my age. After shaking hands Andy pulled his cowboy hat off his head to scratch an itch. I could see that his hair was brown and cut very short. His wide brow and big smile made his face look broad - kind of engaging.

"Nice to meet you Andy," I said with a smile. "I guess we are brothers in the Order."

"I guess so," He returned with a chuckle. "You know, we don't usually let someone join the first night they arrive. We usually wait and choose pretty carefully. Ken said you were just the guy, so you can thank him for signing you up."

I wasn't exactly sure if this was a compliment, but I thought it might be, so I just nodded like I understood and smiled.

Then Maurice walked up to us and said, "You guys going to gab all day? Or are we going to saddle up all these horses?"

It appeared that as the head wrangler, Maurice, was the boss. So Andy got moving and I turned around to see where Ken was; I figured he would give me a clue as to how I could help. When I looked around for Ken I couldn't find him. Then I heard his voice calling from the corral.

"Hey, Harry!" Ken yelled out at me. "Come on out here."

When I saw where the voice was coming from I could see Ken out in the inner corral roping a horse. I went out through the gate that we had used with the truck and headed out to meet Ken who was already holding three horses. When I got there he handed me the rope to one of the horses.

"So you want to know why we wear cowboy boots?" He asked with a smile.

"Yes, I sure do," I replied sincerely.

In retrospect I should have taken a hint from the big grin on Ken's face. At the time I was so earnest in wanting to learn all about horses and how to care for them that my regular self-defense instincts were turned off.

The next thing I knew Ken was simultaneously telling me to hold on to the rope and swatting the rear of the horse to which the rope was attached. I just barely had time to tighten my hands around the rope when I was yanked forward. As I held on for all I was worth the big brown horse trotted off in front of me, my weight dragging on the rope didn't seem to bother the horse at all.

While I was struggling to stay on my feet I could hear Ken laughing uproariously behind me. It never occurred to me that I could just let go of the rope. For all I knew that would be bad for the horse and I didn't want to hurt the horse in any way. So I held on while my legs took large bouncy steps to stay upright.

When Ken felt he had laughed enough he shouted out, "Harry, dig in your heels!"

Ken's instruction wasn't all that easy to put into action. The horse was moving ahead fast enough that my legs were behind me rather than in front of me. I decided that I would have to use the tension on the rope as a kind of handle and jump up in the air throwing both my feet forward.

Determined not to fail I squeezed my grip even tighter on the rope while I jumped up in the air throwing my feet forward. It was kind of like when you do the standing long jump. When my feet landed on the ground I leaned back holding onto the rope and dug in my heels. For awhile it was like water skiing on the heels of my boots, both of my hands were in front of me holding onto the rope and my heels were cutting two grooves into the soft dirt of the corral.

After awhile the horse got the message that it was time to slow down. Soon I was firmly in place and the horse had stopped and was looking back at me as if to say, "Well, it took you long enough!"

Ken then came running up behind me with his two horses in tow.

"That was pretty good, Harry," Ken said, trying to keep from laughing. "Let me show you one more thing that will help."

Ken handed me the ropes of the two horses he was leading and grabbed the rope that I was holding. He then went on to demonstrate how to hold the rope for maximum effect. Holding the rope with his left hand in front towards the horse he wrapped the rope around his rear end and held it with his right hand near his right thigh.

"When you hold the rope like this, lean back and dig your heels in – left foot ahead of the right foot -, it will help you to keep your balance and also apply the most amount of pressure you can for your body size," Ken explained while demonstrating the position.

I could see how his position would allow him to apply pressure while keeping his balance and sliding forward if the horse was pulling hard. Of course, he could have explained this before swatting the horse on the rear, but then I guess that wouldn't have been as much fun!

Just as I was thinking that I now knew the value of the heels on cowboy boots Ken went on to say, "There is another even more important reason to wear cowboy boots when you ride, I'll show you that later."

Since I was holding two horses, Ken went out and got another. With two horses each we headed back to where Maurice and Andy were busy saddling their horses. They had eight horses done by the time we got back and I could see that Maurice was thinking we needed to speed things up.

Ken showed me how to tie the horses up with a bowline knot. Fortunately I had learned this knot in Scouts. He was pretty impressed that I got it right the first time. When our four horses were tied up we went in and got four bridles. Ken showed me how to put the bit into the horse's mouth and attach the leather bridle straps.

"If they try to keep their teeth closed," Ken instructed, "You just stick your thumb into the side of the horses mouth. This will cause him to open up."

I watched as Ken held the bit in position and inserted his thumb into the back, side part of the horse's mouth. It was like a magic password. The horse's mouth just opened right up.

"You bridle up the rest of these and I'll start with the saddles," Ken directed.

Soon we were building up speed. Once our horses were saddled and bridled we moved them to the growing line of horses tied to the corral fence. Then we went to get more. I would bridle the horses and Ken would saddle them. A few of the horses tossed their heads around while I was trying to do my job. Ken never said anything more. He just let me work things out while he threw the saddle blanket and then the saddle on the horse. Ken would then tighten up the cinch that goes under the horse to keep the saddle on.

Before I knew it, we were done. I stood back and counted all of the horses that the four of us had prepared for riding. There were 48 horses lined up on the fence. All were saddled up and ready to go. As we looked at the horses I noticed Maurice was going down the line double-checking the horses and equipment. I watched as he went in between the horses and around the back of them. He was doing just as Ken had suggested to me. He was talking to the horses so that they knew he was there and keeping one hand on the rear end of the horse that he was going behind. Seeing him do this was a perfect lesson for me.

Occasionally one of the horses would get upset with its neighbor and try to bite it or kick at it. That would cause the wrangler closest to the horse causing trouble to call out for that horse to stop. The horses usually did stop. I still wasn't sure if it was just that the horses were done being grumpy, or if the wrangler's voice actually had an affect. In any case, it sure looked like the wranglers knew what they were doing!.

Then I remembered what Ken had said about how the horse's ears would tell if it was happy or angry. So I started watching all the horse's ears; it was amazing. It was like you could read their minds by watching their ears. When I saw one of the horses start trying to bite at a neighbor I immediately looked at its ears. Sure enough, they were laid straight back and flat against the back of his head. As soon as he stopped trying to bite the ears moved back towards the middle. The horses with their ears forward were definitely the most contented. I spent a good ten or fifteen minutes watching all of the horses ears, it was fascinating.

The wranglers were now done getting the horses ready so the four of us gathered in front of the tack house to wait for all of the riders to arrive. Feeling really good about being included in this group, I was soaking up cowboy knowledge as quickly as I could.

Another thing that I learned is that all of the horses had names. Maurice, Andy and Ken called each horse by name as they worked with them. I was amazed that they could remember so many names and which name went with which horse. Gradually I began to pick up that most of the names were connected in some way to either the way the horse looked or the horse's personality. I figured that made it easier to remember the names.

There was a big red horse that was called, Big Red. There was a white horse that was called, Whitey. A horse that couldn't seem to keep his feet still was called, Dancer. A brown horse with a star shaped white patch on its forehead was called, Star. It all started to make sense as I tried to absorbed the sheer volume of horses, names, colors and personalities.

After a while the rest of my fellow campers started filtering down from breakfast. They all kept their distance from the horses. I noticed a few of the boys looking at me with "What are you doing right up next to the horses?" looks, but I acted like I didn't notice. I tried not to be smug about being included with the wranglers, but it was pretty hard not to gloat a little. I did feel pretty good inside. It really wasn't about the others not being included; it was just about me being included. The other wranglers made me feel like they believed in my potential. I really appreciated that. Of course in a few minutes, my riding potential was going to be tested.

I was excited about getting up on a horse and learning to ride, though I was also a bit nervous. I really wanted to do well at this. What if I wasn't able to stay on the horse? What if I couldn't steer it and someone had to lead me around like at the pony ride when I was younger? What if I fell off and got trampled by the horse?

I took a firm grip on my mind and decided that whatever happened, it wasn't going to be because I didn't try my best. So worrying about it wasn't going to do a bit of good.

While I mentally wrestled with myself I noticed that Maruice had gone over to get one of the horses. He led the horse back to where the group was standing and called for everyone's attention. Our short course in "How to ride a horse!" was about to begin.

Chapter 18

"Okay, all you city slickers!" Maurice called out to everyone. "In the next two hours you are all going to become cowboys. How's that sound?" All the boys started to cheer and the horse that Maurice was holding looked around like it was wondering if it had missed anything important.

"Let's start with the most basic rule when being around horses," Maurice went on. "Horses are big so if they step on your toes or kick you it is gonna hurt like heck. To avoid that unpleasant experience keep your feet to the side of the horse and use your hand like this if you are going to walk around the back of a horse." He then went on to demonstrate how to safely walk around the back of a horse.

"Never, under any circumstances come up behind a horse without letting it know you are there before you get into kicking range. Announce yourself by talking to the horse. If you can't think of anything to say, like "I'm here" or "Hey horse, don't kick me!" then just make some noise. Be sure that the horse knows you are there before you get too close. Does everyone understand that?" Maurice asked.

A chorus of yes' rang out so Maurice went on to the next point.

Maurice went on to cover the basics of riding. You always get on the horse from the left side. Insert your left foot into the stirrup and pull yourself up. Once you are on the horse put your right foot in the stirrup. The reins are your steering and stopping controls. Left is left, right is right and back is stop. To get the horse to move forward, relax the reins, give a little kick with your heels into the side of the horse and if you feel to, say a little, "Come on boy" or girl as the case may be.

It sounded easy enough to me, I was raring to go. But it would take some time before I could get on a horse. First, all of the other boys and the adults would have to get mounted. I didn't know this right away, but as Maurice finished his little speech Ken grabbed me by the arm and told me to help him get some horses.

Soon I was bringing horses to Maurice, Andy and Ken who would look at the horse and then look at the group to decide which boy or adult should get that particular horse. They were apparently trying to match up horses with riders by using some secret knowledge that allowed them to discern how proficient any particular rider might potentially be.

Each rider was told the name of their horse and helped to mount it. Once the new rider was on the horse the stirrups on the saddle were adjusted to the length of the rider's legs. The rider was asked to stand up in the stirrups, if there was just a little room between the saddle and the rider's rear end, the stirrups were properly adjusted. After that each new rider was led out into the field and told to sit and wait.

Of course some of the boys couldn't help trying to make their horses move. Apparently the horses had been through this many times before, so many of them were generally uncooperative. Most of the boys just sat and waited. One boy leaned too far over to the side to put his foot back in his stirrup and fell off his horse. He wasn't hurt, since the horse was just standing there - just a bit embarrassed. Andy went over and helped him back up.

Soon there were only four horses left so I waited to see which one would be mine. Ken led me to one of the horses. It was a little smaller than the others, but perked up as soon as we came near. Ken told me, "Harry, this is Sparky. She is one of my horses and I think you will like riding her. She has some spunk, so you have to stay in control. But I have a feeling you're going to be just fine."

Sparky was what you call a bay color; her shiny coat was a deep reddish brown color. Her eyes were full of life and she looked ready to go. I liked her right away. Patting her on the neck and looking her in the eyes I silently asked her to be gentle.

Before I got on Ken showed me how to adjust my stirrups. He said, "Just put your hand in this hole on the top of the saddle and pull the stirrup up into your armpit. That is usually the right distance."

I adjusted the stirrup according to his advice. Lifting my left foot I inserted my boot into the stirrup and pulled myself up by holding onto the saddle horn. Throwing my right leg upward over the back of Sparky I landed softly on the saddle.

Ken's final advice was given while he held onto my left boot as it fit snugly into the stirrup, "See how the high heel of your boot keeps your foot from going through the stirrup?" I looked down and could see that it would be hard for the boot to accidentally go through.

"This is the most important reason to wear cowboy boots when you ride," Ken said seriously. "If your foot falls through the stirrup and you fall off the horse, your foot will get caught and you will be dragged along without being able to get loose."

I had seen men get dragged like that in the movies. I didn't think I wanted to experience that so I was glad that I had cowboy boots on. I looked around at some of the other boys…they didn't have cowboy boots. I felt lucky to have come properly prepared.

As I sat on Sparky and settled my rear end into the saddle I watched Ken get on his horse. Ken's horse, which he also personally owned, looked like a bigger version of Sparky. Ken said that his horse's name was Lady. Lady was the same bay color as Sparky, but she had a white patch on her forehead. She was defenitly one of the better looking horses in the herd.

I was distracted from looking Lady over when I saw how Ken mounted his horse. Instead of putting his left foot in the stirrup he put both hands on the saddle horn while facing the back of the horse. Then he stepped forward with his left foot and threw his right leg up over the top causing him to land on the saddle in one smooth motion. It was right out of the movies - like a pony express rider. I was suitably impressed. I determined that I would have to master that technique as soon as possible.

For the next half hour Maurice, Ken and Andy went around to make sure each of the boys could accomplish the basics of turning right, turning left and stopping. As part of my learning process I followed Ken. Wherever he went I tried to get Sparky to follow. She was quite willing to cooperate, which made it much easier for me. I could see that many of the boys had horses that didn't want to budge an inch from where they were standing, that made learning to ride harder for them.

Soon I was able to turn, start and stop at will. Of course this was all at a walking pace. I could see by watching the other boys that I was doing pretty well in comparison, so even though Sparky was doing most of the work I felt good about how it was going.

Finally, when Maurice felt everyone was ready, he announced that we were going on a trail ride. The group was told to head out in one big line. Andy took the lead and Maurice, Ken and the other adults herded all the boys forward and into the line as needed. I decided to stay in the back of the line so I could watch everything that was going on.

Watching Maurice and Ken maneuver their horses was a beautiful thing to behold. They didn't just walk their horses, they would trot here, turn there, stop, start, turn in a circle, every and any way that was needed their horses responded instantly. They had complete control of their horses and they sat on top their saddles like they were glued to them. I watched how they held their reins in their left hand and did the same myself. I noticed that they leaned back a little with the lower body even when the upper body leaned forward as they were trotting, so I leaned back, even though I wasn't trotting.

They stayed sitting upright and balanced even when their horses moved a little in an unexpected direction. It was like they had gyroscopes in their butts. They just flowed right along with the movements of the horse no matter what happened.

I also noticed that they didn't bounce up and down on the saddle when the horse trotted. A couple of the boys had made their horses trot without permission and I could see them bouncing all over the place. One of them, a boy I didn't know, almost fell off and was only saved because the horse stopped all by itself. I wondered if maybe the horse was getting a backache from all that bouncing. In any case, I could see that the boy was happy it had stopped.

While a few of the boys did laugh at the unfortunate rider I could see that most of the boys were concerned that this didn't happen to them. For myself, I couldn't wait to get trotting; even more exciting would be cantering. Cantering is when the horse is running, but not at their highest speed. After that I would hopefully graduate to galloping, which is running at an even faster speed. The ultimate would be a full-blown run. That is when you let the horse go as fast as it can. I wasn't sure how long it would take me to be ready for such an experience, but I was looking forward to trying.

As our group worked its way through camp and out the other side past the pig pen I allowed myself to end up in the very back of the line. I didn't want to be distracted by all the other guys. Some of them were already talking about sports, fishing and food. I was so absorbed in the experience of riding on Sparky that I didn't want think about anything else. Little did I know that excitement was waiting to find me just a short way down the trail.

Chapter 19

My brother Frank is a natural athlete, I am not. He was an All Star pitcher in Little League, I wasn't even chosen to be on a team for the first three years I tried out to play. It isn't that I am terrible at sports I just don't have what many people would call natural talent. If I want to be better than average at a sport I have to work at it very hard. And since I hadn't yet done a sport that I was interested enough in to work really hard to get good at it, I wasn't very good at any particular sport.

With horseback riding, I knew from the very moment that I sat on Sparky's back that I was going to be good at it. I can't tell you exactly how I knew. It was not a "I hope I'm good at it!" or a "I really want to be good at it!" but it was a place of absolute knowledge that I had inside myself that just recognized that I was already good at it. In some strange way it was like my body already knew how to do this even though I had never done it before. I can't explain it, but as we rode down the trail I just knew that I was completely comfortable.

With each step down the trail I was intensely aware of Sparky's energy and enthusiasm. She wasn't some broken down stable horse, she was young, ready and willing to get moving. She walked with a spring in her step and I could sense that she wished we were up front and not in the back of the line. I could feel myself inwardly reaching out to her to feel what she felt and in some strange way I believed that I could sense a part of her world.

As we rode under the tall aspen trees and along the river I watched Sparky's ears. They moved forward and to the sides as we walked down the trail. I listened intently to connect what I could see and hear to how her ears moved. I found that she reacted to distant noises and occasionally to me as I spoke to her and patted her on the neck.

When the trail curved I could see the heads of other horses. I watched their ears, the gait of their walk, their general attitude. Some of the horses would stop every few yards to grab a quick bite of grass off the side of the trail. This would cause the horse behind to need to slow down. It would also cause the rider to be jerked slightly forward as the stretching of the horses neck would cause the reins to pull forward.

Many of the boys were on big strong horses that were much more in control of the situation than their riders. These horses were very experienced and knew all of the "tricks of the trade". I was to learn that grabbing a bite to eat along the way was one of the more popular "I'm taking control of this situation!" moves that these horses would use on riders that didn't know any better. This grabbing a quick bite trick is what caused things to go terribly wrong after we had been on the trail for about twenty minutes.

During our ride I had noticed a horse four places in front of me. It was a big red horse. Its rider was Tom Phillips. I've known Tom for a number of years. We haven't spent much time together in recent times, but we know each other and are friendly. His horse was stretching its neck out so that Tom would loosen the reins. Then it would reach down and grab a mouthful of grass. Tom wasn't really strong enough to stop it, so the horse would munch for awhile and then reach down for another bite.

Since we weren't going too fast it didn't seem like much of a problem. Unfortunately the fellow behind Tom, Jack Meyers (who was one of Eric Winston's buddies in the push Harry into the river episode), didn't have a lot of control over his horse either. Jack was on a gray horse whose natural pace for walking was faster than Tom's horse, so the gray horse kept running into the back of the red horse when the red horse would stop to grab a mouthful of grass.

I watched this happen several times and took notice of the ears of both horses. The gray horse's ears flickered back and forth in apparent irritation, but the red horse laid its ears straight back and feinted a kick when the gray came too close.

Neither of the boys seemed to know that trouble was brewing. All of the wranglers and adults were further up the line so I couldn't point out the problem to them. I could instinctively tell that one of these times the red horse was going to let loose with a kick. I felt like I had to say something even though I really had no authority or experience to justify it.

I called up to Tom, "Hey Tom, don't let your horse grab grass. Hold his head up and give him a kick when he tries to eat."

Jack immediately turned back to me and yelled, "What do you know about it Fruitgarden? Who put you in charge?"

"Nobody put me in charge Jack, but it doesn't take a brain surgeon to tell that if you don't keep your horse off the butt of Tom's horse your going to get kicked."

"Oh yah, Fruitgarden is now the expert on horses. Let's all do what the Lone Ranger tells us!" Jack said in a deriding voice.

No sooner had Jack got these words out of his mouth than my fears took place. It was as if I had the power of seeing the future. Tom never had a chance to comment on the situation because his horse took that moment to stop for a bite and Jack's horse walked right into the back of it. The big red horse laid its ears back flat on its head and kicked with both back feet.

This kicking action caused the rear end of Tom's horse to lift up. Tom was already leaning forward at this time because his horse had stretched its head down and Tom hadn't loosened his grip on the reins, so Tom began to fall forward. Once he started he tried to grab the neck of the horse, which helped enough that Tom landed on the ground feet first instead of head first. The real problem was with Jack.

Horses are pretty fast when they want to be. They know all about kicking and when it is time to get out of the way. Jack's horse reacted instinctively to the situation by trying to get out of the way of the kick. Jack on the other hand, had no idea what was going on.

When Jack's horse jumped to the side to get out of the way Jack dropped his reins and grabbed onto the saddle horn with both hands. With no one in control of the reins Jack's horse was free to do whatever it wanted. Apparently it decided that this was a good time to end the trail ride and go home.

Even though the trail wasn't very wide the gray horse somehow made room and turned around heading for home. As it headed my way I reached out to grab the reins. Unfortunately the gray was just out of reach.

The whole thing happened so fast that on one hand I didn't have time to think and on the other hand everything slowed down and I became intensely aware of everything that was happening. It was Jack's face as he went by, both hands locked with a death grip on the saddle horn, that spoke loudest to me. His face was a study in terror. As his horse went by picking up speed, Jack yelled with panic in his voice, "Help me!"

I think that all of the cowboy movies that I had watched actually helped me to understand what to do. I had seen runaway stages and riders who lost control of their horses many times. Who hasn't watched with excitement as the hero races after the helpless victim and saves the day?

When I turned Sparky around towards the fleeing horse she seemed to know what I was up to. No sooner had I gotten her pointed in the right direction and loosened the reins then she took off like a shot. I didn't even have to kick her. I had known enough to lean forward as I had seen Ken do the day before. I stood up in my stirrups and with the reins in my left hand I held onto the saddle horn with my right hand.

I knew that really good riders didn't hold onto the saddle horn too often, but I figured, "Hey, this is my first day, give me a break!" That I could even have such a thought shows how quickly the mind can work in a short period of time. And also how strange the mind can be. I mean, what difference did it make whether I held on to the saddle horn or not? You would think that my mind would focus on more important things, like hanging on for dear life!

Sparky was fast. She was so fast that we caught up to Jack on his runaway horse within fifty yards. Once I got there I had to slow down with the reins in my left hand while I reached out with my right hand to grab the reins of Jack's horse. It took me some time to get things synchronized, and it didn't help that Jack was yelling his head off saying, "I'm going to die. I'm going to die. Save me!"

Once I got a firm grip on the reins of the gray horse I pulled back on the reins of both horses. Sparky started to stop immediately. The gray resisted, but fortunately I had a good enough grip that it had to stop. Soon we were standing still. Both horses were breathing hard from their exertion. I could feel between my legs that Sparky was exhilarated by the run and ready to continue.

Jack, on the other hand, was quite relieved for the ordeal to be over. As part of his recovery he was repeating over and over again, "Thank you Harry Fruitgarden! I will never say another bad thing about you. Thank you Harry Fruitgarden! I will never say another bad thing about you. Thank you Harry Fruitgarden! I will never say another bad thing about you."

Jack and I were walking our horses in the direction of the rest of the group when Maurice and Ken came racing up on their horses. Apparently the word of trouble had reached them up front and they raced back to help. When they found us walking sedately back towards the group their faces took on the look of confusion.

They never had a chance to ask any questions because no sooner had they arrived then Jack spewed out the story in excited detail. As Jack spoke with animated arm movements Maurice and Ken looked back and forth at Jack and myself. It seemed to me that Jack embellished a bit, but what the heck, it was a good story.

When the story was finally finished Maurice turned to me and said with a smile, "Not bad for your first day!"

When I looked at Ken he just nodded, then along with a slight shrug of his shoulders, a small smile appeared on his face.

When we caught up with the group everyone was in a small meadow and Jack told the whole story once again. It was kind of embarrassing. It isn't that I mind being appreciated, it is just that, well, all I did was try my best. I don't think that needs any special accolades.

Maurice saved me from further embarrassment by using this as an opportunity to educate the group on what had happened and why. Everyone really listened. Most importantly, he said that if your horse tries to run away with you and pulling back on both reins doesn't work, take both hands and pull on one of the reins as hard as you can. A horse can't run fast if its head is pulled way over to the side.

The rest of the ride that morning passed without major incident. One of the boys got off his horse to pee behind a tree and had trouble getting back on. Another boy complained of having a sore butt. But all in all it was a successful trip and a good time was had by all.

It was only when we got back to camp that I learned two more good lessons about riding and being a wrangler.

Chapter 20

When we arrived back at the corral all of the boys dismounted, tied their horses to the fence and walked off to wash up for lunch in the dinning room. I heard many of the boys groaning with a chuckle about how sore they were from the ride. Several of the kids were walking kind of bowlegged. They looked pretty funny.

Once I was again standing on firm ground I found I was a little sore as well. But I considered it a good feeling. I then spent a minute patting Sparky on the neck and thanking her for the ride. As I looked at all of the horses tied to the fence I had the thought that there sure were a lot of them. Just then Ken came around the corner and said, "Bring some horses with you Harry."

I grabbed the reins of two of the horses and walked them to the tack house. Maurice, Andy and Ken were already unsaddling horses. I quickly caught on to how the process worked and began to help. First was undoing the cinch strap that went under the horse to hold the saddle on. Then saddle and blanket were pulled off and put in the tack house. That being done the horses were led to the gate and the bridle was removed so they could roam freely in the corral.

I could see now that a wrangler's job wasn't done until the horses were taken care of. This was another lesson that I hadn't quite anticipated. And as if the work itself wasn't enough, I could hear the bell ringing for lunch. My mouth immediately prepared itself for food by beginning to squirt water up from underneath my tongue and it continued for some time before it accepted that food wasn't going to be forthcoming quickly.

We kept on working until all of the horses were unsaddled and all of the tack was put away in its place. That was the next lesson I learned, wranglers eat first in the morning, but last at lunch. I assumed that would be the same at dinner when rides were taken in the afternoon.

This thought brought to mind another subject that I had observed soon after arriving at camp. Around here they didn't call lunch, lunch. They called it dinner. They also didn't call dinner, dinner...they called it supper. So they had breakfast, dinner and supper instead of breakfast, lunch and dinner. I wondered why this was? It occurred to me that many people do things differently than the way I was taught to do them. That made me think that the world is a bigger and more varied place then I had ever considered. I mean, it is one thing to read about others being different, but when you are actually with them it really hits home. And this was still within the borders of the United States, I couldn't even imagine people speaking other languages like French or Chinese.

This train of thought led me to thinking about other new words I was hearing. My favorite was "you betcha". This meant: you bet. As in...you are right. Where I came from the word "cool" was used as a catchall affirmation of agreement. Here the word was "you betcha". You betcha the day was hot. You betcha the food was good. You betcha that was a fine horse. You betcha just about anything. And you had to let it stretch out and slur a little, you couldn't pronounce it clearly with precise enunciation. As I rolled "you betcha" off my tongue a few times I found that it had a certain ring to it. I decided that if I was going to be a cowboy, "you betcha" would have to be part of my style.

That thought brought me to another subject. Hats. All of the guys around here wore cowboy hats. I figured that I needed to get one as soon as possible. Of course there were different styles of hats, some were felt and some were a kind of woven material that I didn't recognize. Some hats were tall while others were short. I had seen both wide brim and narrow brim hats. I pondered the subject for some time, wondering which would be best for me.

As I unsaddled horse after horse my mind wandered over being a cowboy from many different angles. I checked out each horse that I unsaddled carefully. I wanted to know the horses: what they looked like, their names and what kind of personality they had. When I was finished with a horse I patted it on the neck and expressed appreciation for that particular horse. I felt like all of these horses were new friends and I wanted to get to know them.

With each passing minute it seemed like I was being transformed into a cowboy, I was talking different and even walking different. The thing that I kept coming back to in my mind was that I liked it. This cowboy stuff was definitely for me.

When all of the horses were free in the corral, we washed up and headed to the dining hall. By the time we got there most of the boys had eaten and were gone to parts unknown. I headed to the counter and grabbed a plate. Finding grilled cheese sandwiches and french fries - I couldn't have been happier.

Even though I had eaten a pretty large breakfast I found that the activities of the morning had made me ravenously hungry. I sat down, waited for Ken, Maurice and Andy to say their prayers and then dug into the food. As we ate, Maurice and Andy discussed chores that they had to take care of in the afternoon: there was a short section of fence to be fixed and a leak in the roof of one of the cabins that had to be looked at.

I was surprised that Maurice and Andy were so independent and able to do jobs that I had always associated with adults. My parents would never have trusted me with those kinds of jobs. Ken said that he had some chores to do for his mother. He wasn't specific about what that meant and I was so busy eating that I didn't ask. Soon the others had left me at the table with a group, "See you later, Harry."

As I sat there finishing up my french fries I pondered the morning's events. It seemed like I had lived a whole week in just one morning. I picked up the last french fry and dipped it in ketchup. As it happened, it was a large french fry, which took some maneuvering to fit it into my mouth. Just as I had managed the job and closed my teeth to a satisfying smushing sensation a voice addressed me from across the table.

"Hello Harry," the voice said with a joyful tone.

I had been so concentrated on eating that I hadn't noticed anyone else in the room. It was a female voice. I looked up and almost choked as my eyes recognized Shannon's face. She was standing right in front of me in jeans and a red blouse. Her face was bright with a big smile. And I was sure that she expected a response from me.

I desperately wanted to say something but my mouth was so full that I was afraid to open it. In the back of my mind I was asking the universe: Why does this keep happening to me? She looked at me with question in her eyes, like: So can you speak?

I was a little worried that I was going to injure my throat or just plain choke, but I swallowed that mouthful with way too few chews. I mentally forced that food into my stomach so that I could speak. Apparently my efforts to swallow were quite obvious. She took pity on me and said, "Oh, I see, you've got your mouth full of food." Then she laughed.

That gave me just the time that I needed to recover from my record breaking swallowing attempt. I took a quick sip of water to make sure the pipes were clear and then squeaked out a, "Oh, hi. Yah, I was just finishing up lunch…I mean dinner."

"Lunch?" Shannon asked with an incredible twitch of her eyebrows.

"Sorry," I squeaked. "I'm used to calling lunch, lunch. I mean dinner... lunch. I mean, what you call dinner, I am used to calling lunch."

Even though I had just been thinking about this subject I had trouble getting my thoughts out. Shannon's presence seemed to have a devastating effect on my thinking process.

"Oh," she said. "I have heard that some people call dinner lunch. But we have always called it dinner. So it is strange when people call it lunch. Of course I am sure that there are people who call it other things, but I don't know what those other things might be…."

As Shannon spoke I became mesmerized by her voice and face. I completely lost contact with what she was saying. I just sort of merged with the feeling that I liked being in her presence. Beyond that, I was completely unable to function.

The next thing that I knew I was being asked another question. I had to force myself to understand what was being said. "So, Harry, would you like to help me do the dishes?" Shannon was asking me. Once again she was wearing a beautific smile.

The question was so unexpected that it took me some time to figure out what it meant. Help? Dishes? With Shannon? Once I started to comprehend the true meaning of her question I couldn't help asking myself: Do cowboys do dishes? As I looked at her the fireworks in my head gave me the definitive answer to that question: Who cares what cowboys do or don't do? You have just been invited to spend some time with this incredibly beautiful girl. Buck yourself up and get things going here.

Finally after what must have seemed like an eon to her I was able to squawk out a feeble, "Sure, I'll help."

Chapter 21

It isn't that I have never spent time talking to girls. I had made small talk with girls any number of times. It is just that Shannon had some kind of strange affect on me. I had verbally sparred with countless boys, and both male and female adults, so to find myself tongue-tied in her presence was new and disorienting. This was especially true since I had always considered my ability to talk my way out of difficult situations to be one of my strongest talents.

We started our dishwashing session by adding my plate and glass to the large pile that had been left from all of the campers. Normally the thought of washing this many dishes would have put a frown on my face, but as I looked at the huge stack of dishes I couldn't help grinning from ear to ear. It's funny how the same task can look different when you change your point of view.

Shannon noticed my smile and asked, "What's put such a big smile on your face?"

Oh, boy. Here I was, not 30 seconds into it and I was already in deep trouble. How could I tell her what I was really feeling? At the same time, how could I lie to her?

Once again time slowed down in my mind. Thoughts swirled right and left. I pondered a whole list of questions:

What would the popular guys in school do?

What would my brother (who is popular with girls) do?

What would my mother or father suggest?

What do movie stars do in situations like this? I even flashed a "What would Babe Ruth do?" through my mind. I was desperate. I had to come up with a solution to this dilemma right here and now.

At the end of my list I finally came to what I realized was the most important question. Who am I? I am not any of those other people. What kind of person do I want to be?

I knew instantly what kind of person I had to be in order to have Shannon as a true friend. The reality of what I knew to be true was so strong that I blurted out my answer before caution or doubt could stop it.

I looked right into Shannon's eyes and said, "I am grinning because normally the thought of doing this many dishes would depress me for a week, but the thought of doing them with you put a smile on my face."

Ahh…the sweet magic of truth.

I watched Shannon's eyes as she absorbed my words. I had the satisfaction of seeing them flash from recognition, surprise, blush, the grasping of firm control, and finally, a coy smile with both eyes and lips. Where girls learn this stuff I don't know, but she instantly knew what to do with my confession of truth.

"Well," she said as if I had announced that blue rather than pink wallpaper should have been placed on the walls of a redecorated room, "Let's get to it!"

The next hour of washing was pleasantly stretched to an hour and a half. We talked comfortably and with animation about whatever came to mind. We rambled from where we lived and what we liked to do, to her family and mine. I learned that Shannon is Ken's sister. She is about six months younger than I am, while Ken is about seven months older than me. They live in Arizona during the winter and run the camp during the summer.

I told Shannon a few of my escapades on the way to camp. She particularly liked the mummies in the bus prank. She had already heard about the morning's horse adventure. She asked me for details and I told her what had happened. She then stopped her washing for a moment and looked at me eye to eye.

"You know, you have made quite an impression on the guys around here," she said.

No, I didn't know. So I asked, "What do you mean?"

Shannon responded by saying in a somewhat conspiratorial voice, "Well, I heard Ken say that he had never seen anything like it. The way you were just sort of "there" to help this morning, and how you seem to know how to be around horses even though you haven't been around them. And how you ride like you know how to ride, yet you say you never have ridden a horse before."

I couldn't help blurting out, "I told Ken I was on a pony ride once!"

My pitiful comment made Shannon laugh. "You are funny, Harry," she said.

I liked making her laugh, but this was a subject that I myself was trying to understand more fully, so I continued on with my thoughts.

"Well, I can't explain it," I went on. "When I was riding Sparky it just sort of felt like home. It was like I had been there before, but not in a long time."

Shannon looked at me while I made this confession. Her eyes seemed to be looking within me as I spoke. Then she said with a simple honest wisdom that made me appreciate her even more, "Special talents come from God, so don't let it swell your head."

What talents coming from God meant was something I would need to ponder further. The idea that my ability to ride was from some hidden place did make sense, but I wasn't sure how it could be true. Not letting things swell my head I understood right away, I didn't want to be that kind of person. I nodded my agreement to her.

My conversation with Shannon over the dishes had been a heartfelt sharing between two people. It was simple and without hidden messages, just open honest sharing. I had never done that with a girl - or with anyone for that matter. When talking with guys, one's image is often more important than how you truly feel. With Shannon I felt like I could share who I really am. She would accept me without judging me harshly like my parents might. I felt like I had made a true friend.

How it is that girls can keep guys constantly off balance is something that I haven't yet figured out. As we finished up the dishes I had thoughts of spending more time with Shannon, but I was to find suddenly that my view of the future was just a fantasy.

As the last dish was laid to rest Shannon took off her apron and looked at me for a moment. She smiled. I smiled. Then, like a mysterious fairy that has unknowable things to do she sprung up and flitted out the door with a parting, "See you later Harry!"

I didn't even have time to finish my mental "When?" before she was gone and out of sight. It was instantly like the light had left the room. Suddenly I was in an old kitchen with cracked linoleum and stained counters. The smell of dish soap and the buckets of pig slop invaded my nostrils. I hadn't even noticed these things when

Shannon was in the room. I walked quickly out of the kitchen and back through the dining hall to head for the bunkhouse.

I found the bunkhouse and the general environs of camp to be deserted. Where everyone had gone to I had no idea. For a moment it struck me as odd that no adults were concerned about my whereabouts. Then I was filled with the realization that I was in the mountains of Colorado with no one looking over my shoulder. I had just spent an hour and a half with a beautiful girl and the sun was shining bright and hot, it was an incredible realization of how beautiful life could be.

In a flash of intuitive understanding I knew what I should do. I put on my swimsuit, grabbed my towel and headed for the river. I didn't point myself towards the bridge where others might find me; I walked upstream through the forest until I found a private spot with just the right mix of sun, shade, and a little swimming hole. It was perfect.

I took a moment to look around before I went in the water. The sky was a deep blue with just a few wispy white clouds. The forest was thick with pine trees and their scent was strong. I could hear the buzzing of insects mixing with the sound of rushing water from the river. You could see the rocks under the surface of the water as clearly as through glass. Everything was clean and fresh. It was wondrously beautiful.

As I stepped into the water my feet were invigorated by the cold water. It took me some time to get used to the chill, but once I did it was refreshing. I was in a spot where the water was about three feet deep. The current was swift, but not so strong that I couldn't hold my position. As I looked into the water I noticed some large rocks on the bottom. The position of the rocks gave me an idea.

Facing upstream I filled my lungs with air and submerged myself in the water. Reaching down towards the two rocks I grabbed them firmly and let my legs float freely behind me. By using my arms I could then raise and lower my body. I could also angle a little to the left and right. It was as if I was flying like superman underwater. Of course I had to come up for air more often than I would have liked, but it was lots of fun to fly underwater.

For a good ten or fifteen minutes I experimented with my underwater flight. Then I propped myself up on the side of the stream and threw rocks into the little waterfalls that were caused by some of the larger boulders further out in the river. When I started to feel chilled by the water I lay down on my towel and bathed in the warm sun.

As I lay relaxed and at peace on the side of the river I began to mentally unwind. This was a practice that I had used for some time. I would take a few deep breaths and then consciously try to empty my mind of restless thoughts. I found that the breathing helped me to pull away from all of the clutter that gathered in my head. I don't remember how I discovered this, but I did like the results.

It was like I had to process all of the things that had been going on in my life, so that I could sort everything out and put it all in a good perspective. I found that even if I didn't come to any firm conclusions about what to do with my observations it still helped to mull them over. Often I found that these sessions led to possibilities that I hadn't previously considered.

Once I felt calm I began to review the day. I was amazed to find how much had taken place. When I got to Jack and the runaway horse I mentally relived the experience. As I went through each detail I realized that my most powerful impression was not that I had saved Jack and been the hero, it was the powerful presence of Sparky and my feeling of being in harmony with her. It had been like we were connected in some internal way. I was intensely aware of the power and intelligence that had been flowing through her. I could feel right through her to the ground that she pounded with her hooves. I had somehow instinctively known what to do and how to do it. My body had just done what my mind didn't technically know how to do. It was both inexplicable and wonderful.

Shannon's comment about this being a gift from God was another big question. When I had prayed for a hole-in-one on the miniature golf course and actually hit one I had to admit that that could have been a gift from God. But I hadn't done any praying about riding horses. How or why would God give me a gift that I didn't ask for? And exactly what did a gift from God mean? Did that mean I was going to be some kind of super cowboy without even trying? And if so, what was the purpose of that? It seemed to me that while it was nice to be good at something easily, learning and struggling to be good at something was just as important as actually being good at it. Although once again, why this should be so I wasn't exactly sure.

When I had mulled these thoughts over for a while I finally got to the Shannon part of my day. It had been nice to hear that the wranglers were feeling good about having me around. But the most important part of the afternoon had been that time spent with Shannon. I smiled as I lay there thinking about her. Her face was radiant and her hands moved like the conductor of a symphony. She walked like a sprightly dancer. Her voice was like the music of.... Soon my smile faded into a pleasant slumber and I melted into peace until an unexpected clamor woke me.

Chapter 22

My pleasant nap on the side of the river was brought to an end by shouting and yelling that I couldn't immediately locate. I sat up to see if I could tell where the commotion was coming from. It didn't seem to be coming from the forest. Apparently it was coming from upstream and it was getting closer. I couldn't quite grasp how that could be.

The next thing I knew screams of delight were upon me. I could see fellow campers floating down the river on rafts and inner tubes. All the guys were bobbing up and down as they floated over the small rapids. They were yelling and splashing at each other. They were like a swarm of strange creatures that had appeared from nowhere.

Now I knew where everyone had gone off too. Then I remembered the group was supposed to go fishing. I guess their plans changed. For a moment I felt a pang of "Why didn't they invite me?" Then I remembered what I had been doing and they hadn't - that put a smile on my face. One of the boys noticed me sitting on the bank of the river and everyone started pointing and shouting. It was all very friendly except for Eric Winston

- he glared at me, trying to give me the evil eye as he floated by.

Rafting down the river looked like a lot of fun. I started to think I should ask Ken about taking a rafting excursion, but thinking of Ken made me wonder about the time, I wanted to be at the corral in time to help feed the horses. Then it occurred to me that all the boys would be returning to the bunkhouse to change after arriving back at camp. If I ran I could probably beat them back and disappear before they arrived, so I put on my boots – which looked pretty funny with swim trunks - jumped up and ran through the forest.

I didn't look for a trail; I just headed off in the general direction of the bunkhouse. I dashed through the trees like a skier going through a slalom course. It reminded me of when I ran down the hill at Crescent Lake, except there I had been on a fairly steep slope, here it was flat. I ducked branches, dodged fledgling trees and jumped old dead trees that had come to rest on the forest floor.

I found that my legs were a bit sore from the morning's ride, but the cold water of the river had helped. I felt alive and free. I ran with enthusiasm and abandon. I even let loose with a couple of unfettered whoops of pure enjoyment.

I don't know why I should feel so comfortable in the forest. As a city boy I hadn't spent much time in the wild. Although I seemed to have a good sense of direction because when I came out of the trees I was just yards from the bunkhouse.

Soon I was once again tucked into my cowboy boots and heading for the corral. When I got there all of the horses were milling around, they hadn't been taken to the far pasture like the previous day. A number of the horses perked up when they saw me, but they quickly lost interest when they realized that I wasn't bringing dinner…I mean supper. Well, I don't suppose the horses care what it is called.

Climbing over the fence I decided that I wanted to get in amongst the horses. I walked over to the edge of a group of about ten horses and slowly made my way in closer. I spoke to them as I approached. At first a couple of horses trotted away when I got too close. When I reached a horse that was a reddish orange color that is called sorrel, I was allowed to come up close and pat his neck.

He was curious about me and sniffed my shirt. I put my hand in front of his nose they way you do with dogs so they can sniff you. His nostrils flared wide and his eyes looked at me with a "You got any food?" look. He then quivered his lips and his tongue came out and licked at my palm. I had been licked by cats and dogs before, but never a horse. His tongue was big and wide. It wasn't as bristly as a cat's. I was careful to keep my fingers away from his teeth. I liked that he felt comfortable enough with me to do this.

As he licked my palm I could feel the softness of the skin around his nose. Horses have hairs like whiskers in that area too, some of them were a bit prickly. With my right hand I patted his neck and watched his ears. They were forward, so I knew he was feeling comfortable.

Another horse came over to see what was going on. It was a big tan color called buckskin. The buckskin colored horse moved right in and I saw the sorrel's horse's ears move to the side position and flicker momentarily to the back position. I patted his neck and told him to be nice. That seemed to distract him enough that I could extend my other hand to the buckskin. Soon I had two horses licking a hand each.

That is what I was doing when Maruice, Ken and Andy drove up in the truck. Hearing them arrive I excused myself from my two new friends and went to open the gate. Once the truck was through the gate I closed it and jumped up to help distribute the hay.

I had seen Ken and Andy looking at each other when they noticed I had been out with the horses. They didn't say anything to me, but I could tell that they were just kind of wondering what I was up too. So I spilt the beans to see what they would say.

"I was just out saying hello to those horses and they started licking my palms. Why would they do that?" I asked Ken and Andy.

"Did you give them something to eat?" Andy asked.

"No, " I replied. "I was just being friendly."

"Well," Ken said. "They were probably going after the salty flavor on your skin. They like salt. We leave a big block of salt out for the horses to lick when they feel like it. "

As we pushed hay over the side of the truck I asked another question. "So, why are some horses nice and easy to get along with and others aren't?"

Both Ken and Andy laughed for a few moments and then Ken said, "Horses are like people, they have personalities. Some are naturally nice and some are grumpy. Some are made grumpy by people who don't treat them very well."

Ken went on to say, "Horses have a keen sense of the intent of people. They seem to be able to feel if a person is going to treat them well or not. So if they get along with you easy it means that you are in some way saying silently to them, I'm an okay person."

I nodded my head that I was listening and absorbing what Ken said. I was thinking about people who you could just tell by looking at them that they weren't very nice or that they would be a friendly person. So I figured it must be like that for horses - although exactly how that would look to a horse I couldn't quite imagine.

Then I thought that the sun is the same no matter who it shines on. And it doesn't matter how anyone or anything sees the sun. Once they learn to read the sun's brightness through the filter of their viewing system the end result is the same. They open their eyes wider or the squint them narrower as they need. It is the same for people. Once you learn to read people you can tell pretty quickly if they are going to be a nice person. Horses had their own way to do this and they seemed to be pretty good at it.

When we were done feeding the horses, we went back to wash up and have dinner…I mean supper. When I got into the supper line the hall was packed with animated kids talking about the day's adventures. I got a few pats on the back for saving Jack. I heard one small group talking about how much fun the rafting trip was. One fellow was saying that his butt was so sore he didn't know if he would ever be able to sit normally again. That comment caused some good natured laughing and nods of agreement.

When I got my food Shannon was nowhere to be seen - I looked right away to find her. When I got my desert of chocolate pudding from Mrs. Hutchins, she asked me to come see her after supper was over, that made me nervous. All of my "you are in trouble again" radar went into full alert. It was hard to enjoy my desert after that. I couldn't imagine what I had done to get into trouble. I racked my brain for anything that I might have done that would cause offense, I just couldn't think of anything. Everything had been going so well.

I dipped into a negative whirlpool of thought as I picked slowly at my pudding. I started to think about how everything always goes wrong and how life can be so unfair. And how no one really understands me or cares about me.

By the time I was done with dinner I was a mental wreck. My stomach was turning flips and my mind was racing all over the place with nowhere to go except down. I couldn't help asking myself: How do I keep getting myself into these stuations?

The dinning hall was pretty much cleared of people and as I placed my plate on the pile of dirty dishes I decided I may as well face the music and get it over with.

Mrs. Hutchins was in the back of the kitchen rustling through some bags, apparently she had been to town for supplies that afternoon. I could see cases of this and that which still hadn't been put away.

"Mrs. Hutchins?" I called out in not much more than a whisper. I guess I was hoping she wouldn't hear me and I could say that I had tried and then somehow escape without being noticed.

"Be right there Harry," She replied instantly.

She certainly wasn't hard of hearing. This made me even more nervous. I guess a little bit of deafness would have made me feel that she was potentially not as strong as I feared. But no such luck was to be had by me, she was in fully capable form and I was about to receive her fury.

"Ah, here it is," I heard Mrs. Hutchins say.

Without any preamble, Mrs. Hutchins turned around and presented me with the item that she had been looking for: it was a brand new cowboy hat.

I was stunned. I mean floored. I mean flabbergasted. I mean I was totally speechless. It was all I could do to reach out my hands and receive it. I simply couldn't believe it. I looked up at Mrs. Hutchins with what she apparently understood was a "really for me?" look. She said with a big smile, "Yes, Harry, for you."

I looked back at the hat and just stared at it like it was an ancient relic not to be jostled lest it break. It was a tan color with a brown band around the base where the brim was attached. It was absolutely perfect.

"I hope it is the right size," Mrs. Hutchins was saying. But I had trouble hearing her, for some unknown reason water was gushing out of my eyes and I was having trouble breathing.

"Do you like it?" Mrs. Hutchins was asking, but I couldn't respond I was too busy melting into a puddle of mush.

Then Mrs. Hutchins took a good look at me and saw what was happening. Experienced mothers understand these things no matter whose child is at hand, she smiled and opened her arms. I stepped forward and felt embraced by the mother of all.

It took me some time to recover. Fortunately none of the boys were there to see me. There were only a few kitchen staff around to see what was happening and they left us respectfully alone.

We stood there for a few minutes while I slowly came back to my senses. This spontaneous act of buying me a hat was such a perfect expression of caring and so in tune with me as a person that it was overwhelming to me. I wasn't even sure that she realized how meaningful this was to me. I suspect that she had seen plenty of kids come through camp over the years. She probably knew much more about what was going on then I could ever imagine. Oh, heck, I had no idea about what she did or didn't know. I just knew that this was one of the best gifts that I had ever received in my life.

Finally I was able to breathe normally and the water had ceased to flow from my eyes. Mrs. Hutchins handed me a napkin to fix my face. When I was done wiping and drying she said, "Try it on Harry. Let's see if it fits."

With both hands I ceremoniously placed the hat on my head. It went on like it had been made just for my head. It was perfect. I looked up at her to see what she thought. As if her smile wasn't enough, she said, "You look mighty fine, Harry."

I beamed. Somehow I knew that she spoke the truth. This hat looked right on me. I felt it. I knew it.

When I started to say thank you my eyes began to percolate water again. Mrs. Hutchins stopped me midstream and said, "I know how you feel, Harry. I'm glad I could do this for you."

I gave Mrs. Hutchins another quick hug. It was a little awkward because the hat was still on my head, but I wasn't about to take it off. Then I let her go and turned to leave. Just as I was about to walk away a face popped in through the back door. I turned towards the door to see Shannon looking right at me. She smiled and said, "Nice hat Harry!" Then she was instantly gone out the door again.

I was about to move again when Ken came bouncing into the kitchen through the back door. He looked up, saw me and without pause said, "Hey, nice hat Harry, want to help me slop the pigs?"

I looked at Mrs. Hutchins and she nodded a yes. So I went over and grabbed a couple of buckets. A few steps later Ken and I were out the door and heading for the pigpen, things were back to normal.

After we were done feeding the pigs I once again attended the evening program. There was singing, a couple of skits and Jonesy told a fairly long story about a haunted cabin in the forest. I got a few compliments on my hat from some of the boys. Eric Austin tried to trip me, but failed. I didn't see Shannon. All-in-all it was a pretty low key ending to a day that had been over full with action and emotion.

When I thought about the fact that this was just my first full day at camp I had a momentary flash of concern about being able to handle the intensity of the next seven weeks. I was used to 'living on the edge" in my life. But I was also used to plenty of time by myself. As I went to sleep that night I silently hoped that my life would find some kind of balance that included both excitement and peace.

Chapter 23

Fortunately for my mental equilibrium, life at the Circle H Ranch settled into a routine that fit me like a glove. I rose early to help with the horses and almost every day I rode Sparky. Some days we went on long trail rides for up to six hours or more. It became my job to ride at the back of the line and help boys that were having trouble keeping up. My comfort as a rider began to settle in so deeply that I couldn't remember ever not being able to ride.

Sometimes it would rain as we rode out on the trail. We would all wear dark green waterproof ponchos. Even though the ponchos had hoods I would always wear my hat. It became my trademark. No one ever saw me without that hat.

I spent so much time with Sparky that she became completely comfortable with me. She was the perfect blend of calm when stopped and ready to go once we started moving. Everyone became so accustomed to me riding around on her that sometimes I would saddle her up by myself and just go for a ride. It amazed me that I was given such freedom. I was so appreciative of this opportunity that I did everything that I could to maintain my good graces with Mr. and Mrs. Hutchins and the other adults at camp.

In secret I began to practice the pony express horse mounting technique that Ken often used. I had watched him carefully and one day when no one was around I rode Sparky to a secluded spot and tried it.

My first attempt was pretty bad if I do say so myself. It was a good thing that no one had been looking. I grabbed the saddle horn, tried to swing my right leg up and over, but only got about halfway up and fell to the ground in a heap. Sparky just turned her head to look at me. I could imagine her thinking, "That was really pitiful!"

After climbing back up to my feet I tried to figure out what the problem was. Well, not exactly. I knew what the problem was: I couldn't do it! What I tried to figure out was: What is the solution?

I finally decided to break the whole action down into parts. I spent several sessions focusing on my hands and arms. Then I worked on the first step with my left foot while coordinating it with my arms. After that I concentrated on the big swing with my right leg. Each time I worked on it I would end my session with an attempt to put the whole thing together, but no matter how hard I tried I just couldn't get everything happening in a way that allowed it to work.

One day my practice session was ended early because I almost made it. What I mean is that after several attempts I was getting higher and higher as I swung my right leg up. Only the first time I swung my right leg up high enough that it started to go over the back of the saddle, I thought for a split second that I was going to make it; unfortunately my premature celebration caused me to loose focus. My momentum to go over the saddle stopped and I came crashing down on the back edge of the saddle in a way that guys don't like to land.

It took me a few minutes to recover. It was a pain that I had never experienced before and hope never again to experience.

It is a testament to my determination that I didn't give up. I knew that I could do it; I just couldn't quite make that last transition to up and over. Several times I had made it most of the way up, only to slide off the side unable to conquer those last few inches. There was some little thing that I couldn't quite get right but I wasn't sure what it was.

One day I found myself in front of the lodge with Sparky. I was just standing there ready to mount up and head for the corral when Ken, Andy, Mr. and Mrs. Hutchins and Shannon all appeared on the porch. I know I wouldn't have tried it if Shannon hadn't been there, but it was such a perfect moment to unveil my secret that I decided that I should go for it. There is nothing like a pretty girl to make a young guy feel like he can conquer the world!

It was now success or complete humiliation, I was fully committed. I waited for the conversation to ebb. Finally I was noticed and Ken asked me what I was up to. I said that I was heading down to the tack house. Everyone was looking at me. Then I looked at Shannon and smiled. When she smiled back I went for it.

I grabbed the saddle horn, faced the back of Sparky - which happened to be in a perfect position to give my audience a good view - and swung my right leg up and over the top.

It was perfect.

I landed squarely on top of the saddle and nonchalantly turned Sparky so that I could face the small group. I took a quick moment to appreciate several of the mouths that had become slightly opened with surprise and the twinkle of delight in Shannon's eyes. Then I touched the brim of my hat in salute and turned Sparky's head toward the tack house. With the slightest nudge of my heels Sparky began to trot forward. I sat straight up and held the reins in a relaxed position with my left hand. I tried to look like a person without a care in the world. My butt never left the surface of the saddle. I had attained gluedness.

While gluedness isn't a technical term - in fact most people don't even recognize it as any kind of word - it definitely describes one of the signs of a person that can ride well in western style. I had attained the ability to keep my butt on the saddle even though the horse was trotting. I didn't need to look back to know that eyebrows were raised and a couple of jaws had dropped a little lower.

And so my reputation as a competent rider grew. I began to ride horses besides Sparky - even though she was always my favorite. In the eyes of many of the old campers and all of the new campers, I was a wrangler. Out on the trail riders listened to me when I said something. It was a new experience for me to be listened to and actually be respected by others.

It wasn't long before I was a better rider than most of the adults that accompanied the campers on trail rides. There were certain horses that were considered the better horses, they had more spirit and thus were harder to handle than most of the horses that inexperienced riders rode. Adults that knew how to ride wanted to ride the better horses. When I wasn't riding Sparky I would usually ride one of these better horses. There were several times that I got into conflicts with adults who felt they should ride the more spirited horses instead of me. Most of the time I backed down, even though it wasn't my nature to do so, I realized that I had a good thing going and it wasn't worth it to rock the boat. One of the times I didn't back down got me into a bit of hot water.

When I had been at camp for just over three weeks I went out with a group of about thirty riders with just two adults. I was the only regular wrangler on the ride. We rode out to a meadow that was maybe twenty minutes walk from camp. The plan was to have a game of "Capture the Flag" on horseback. The idea is that each team has a flag and you can tag people on the opposite team when they come on to your side of the field to try and capture your flag. The game is over when someone gets the opposite team's flag and rides it back across the mid-field line. If a player is tagged by the defending side then the player goes to jail until rescued by another member that comes over and tags them to free them. Playing this game on horseback adds a whole new dimension to the game.

I knew from experience that if I had a good horse my team had a better than average chance of victory. The fact was that on the right horse I could literally ride circles around most of the other riders. So when I heard that we were going to play capture the flag I made sure that I got one of the better horses. When one of the adults complained to me I just rode away on the horse. There really wasn't anything he could do about it.

Well, the team that I was on did win, but the adult went and complained to Mr. Hutchins. That night right before the evening program Mr. Hutchins pulled me aside.

Mr. Hutchins started the conversation with, "I heard your team won at capture the flag today."

"Yes, we did," I replied with a smile.

Mr. Hutchins voice held no tone of accusation. He was completely friendly. He wasn't acting like my buddy, but he was acting like he cared about me and my life.

"I heard about the game because Mr. Johnson told me about it," Mr. Hutchins continued.

Mr. Hutchins' mention of Mr. Johnson sent up an alarm flag in my head. I knew instantly that I was going to be called out on the carpet for taking the horse that Mr. Johnson wanted. Though, I was a little confused because Mr. Hutchins' tone was still warm and friendly. I was used to adults yelling at me when they thought I had done something wrong.

"You've become a good rider in a very short time Harry; better than most of the adults," Mr. Hutchins said. His vocal tone wasn't one of praise. It sounded like he was just observing something that he knew to be true - like the water is wet or the ground is dirty.

I was waiting for things to turn toward what I had done wrong. When it arrived I was a bit surprised because it came in a way that I didn't expect.

"Harry," Mr. Hutchins said looking right into my eyes, "being a good rider in life is not just about how well you can sit on a horse."

He let me ponder his words for a moment. Then he stepped from in front of me and stood to my right. He put his left arm around my back and rested his hand on my shoulder. He didn't say anything for maybe a minute. Then in a soft voice he said, "I think that maybe you shouldn't go riding tomorrow Harry. Why don't you go to the Reservation on that swimming trip tomorrow?"

I didn't say a word, I just nodded ascent. Yes, I would go swimming tomorrow instead of riding. With a little squeeze of my shoulder Mr. Hutchins looked at me with a warm smile and walked away.

I didn't really pay much attention to the program that evening. I was thinking about what had happened with Mr. Hutchins. It wasn't that I thought he was wrong and had treated me unfairly. On the contrary, I was trying to fully absorb how right he was.

Of course I shouldn't have taken the horse the way I did. I knew it was wrong but I did it anyway; I couldn't seem to help myself. I had certainly gotten in trouble plenty of times in the past, so being punished was something that I understood. What I wasn't used to was the fact that Mr. Hutchins didn't really punish me. He didn't say I had to go swimming - as if going swimming was some kind of punishment! He didn't even say that I had done anything wrong. He just pointed out that there was an issue and that I should consider how I wanted to handle it. And he made it not just about taking the horse, but about how I want to live my life in general. That really made an impression on me.

Most incredible to me was that he was showing me the respect of believing that I would want to take responsibility for my own life and make good decisions. Rather than trying to force me to live from his point of view, he was sharing his view with me and believing that I would do something good with it.

When he put his arm around me I had known that he was saying that he cared about me and that he wasn't mad at me, but concerned about me. I really appreciated that. I wasn't used to getting respect and caring from adult men, it felt pretty good - although it did strike me as unfortunate that I had to get into trouble to receive it.

Just as I was stepping outside the lodge that night Shannon appeared out of the darkness and pulled me aside. We went around the back of the lodge where no one would see us. I got the definite impression that she was sneaking out to see me.

"Are you okay Harry?" Shannon asked with genuine concern.

"Yes, sure, why wouldn't I be?" I responded. I could just barely see by the moonlight that there was some surprise on her face.

"Well, I heard that you were in some kind of trouble about taking a horse and that my father was going to have a talk with you," Shannon said to support her reason for concern.

As Shannon spoke it began to dawn on me that she really cared that I was okay. She had sneaked out into the dark to find me and make sure I was all right. I was thrilled. Who could have guessed that getting into a bit of trouble would have such positive results?

Then I noticed that in order to pull me aside Shannon had grabbed my hand and she was still holding it. Suddenly my whole brain was in my hand and sensations of incredible intensity were shooting up my arm. A grin of humongus proportions lit up my face.

Shannon immediately noticed my smile and asked, "Why are you smiling?"

I was too busy enjoying this to say anything so I just stood there and grinned.

Apparently it was infectious because she started to smile too and asked me again, "Why are you smiling?"

Instead of saying anything I just held up my hand with hers in it. She looked at the hands suspended in the air for a short moment and then looked at me with a big grin of her own. I couldn't tell for sure but I think she might have blushed slightly. I know that she didn't let go of my hand, so I figured things were looking pretty good.

We stood there in the darkness for a few minutes. We didn't talk, we just looked up at the sky, the moon, the stars and each other. After a while we heard some noises around the other side of the lodge.

Shannon said, "I've really got to go." Before I could say anything she gave my hand a quick squeeze and flitted off into the darkness.

That was the second squeeze that I had received that evening. They were both intensely meaningful to me. Once again I wondered why these special moments had to be the result of getting into trouble. It was a mystery to me.

The next morning after feeding the horses and having breakfast I joined a group of about fifteen boys who were going to swim at the recreation center on the Ute Indian Reservation. Once again I had no idea that the new day would bring more unexpected adventures.

Chapter 24

Our group of swimmers piled into a large van and we headed off towards the city of Cortez and the Ute Indian Reservation. I hadn't left camp in a car for some time. It struck me as simultaneously strange and amazing that I had become used to thinking horse travel was the norm.

As we made our way down the road I was of two minds about the trip. On one hand I was already missing being on horseback; on the other hand, I was excited about going to the Reservation. The man I had seen at Four Corners, the caves at Mesa Verde and the dreams that came with them, all came back to my mind. I was interested to see what I might learn about the American Indian culture. I felt some kind of inner connection to the Indian people but I didn't know exactly what that meant.

In less than an hour we passed a sign that said we were entering the Ute Indian Reservation. Jonesy was our driver on this trip and I sat up in the front of the van with him. I found him to be an easy going and friendly person. He got along with everyone, both adults and kids. He was a good singer, could play the piano well, cook up a feast out on the trail and he was also a very good storyteller. He is one of those adults that kids don't have any trouble talking too.

I had observed that he gave everyone his full attention and respect. He took a discussion with one of the young campers just as seriously as he did when speaking with other adults. He seemed to know that kids need to be cared about and respected just as much as older people.

As I sat back and adjusted my hat every once in awhile, I asked Jonesy, "So what is the deal with the Ute Indian Reservation?"

Jonesy responded in true storyteller fashion, "Well Harry, many years ago the United States Government made all of the Indians move onto Reservations. The government basically looked around for land that no one else would want and told the Indians to go live there. "

Jonesy's voice carried into the back of the van and more quickly than one would have expected all of the other kids were listening with full attention.

"The Indians lived there for many years pretty much left alone to fend for themselves, " Jonsey continued. "Only that all changed when the government discovered the value of uranium."

"What does uranium have to do with the Ute Indians?" I asked.

"Well, it just so happens, " Jonesy said with a little chuckle, "After searching all over the country the government found that they had given the Ute Indians some of the very best uranium mines. So then they had to pay the Indians in order to mine the uranium. Now all of the Indians receive money from the government in exchange for the uranium."

That sounded like a classic shoot yourself in the foot situation, but I had trouble feeling sorry for the government. From all that I had learned about it in school

176

the American Indians had gotten a pretty raw deal from our country. The Indians that hadn't been killed were rounded up and sent to live where no one would have to look at them, that didn't seem right to me.

"All of this has been pretty hard on the Indian culture," Jonesy then said. "A lot of the young people are having trouble living with both the old Indian traditions and the new influences of White people. This recreation center we are going to is a place where Indians can go for swimming and other sports activities."

I sat quietly digesting Jonsey's explanation of the situation. I knew that I didn't have all of the facts, but I couldn't help feeling that the Indian's had been wronged.

A few minutes later we entered a residential area with small houses lined up in a few rows. There was only dirt surrounding the houses. There were no trees and no signs of toys or swings in the yards. I saw a few broken down cars and a truck or two, this did not look like a happy place to live.

Soon we drove up to what looked like a fairly new building, it was quite large. When we arrived inside it smelled and looked like the local YMCA that I had been to in California, only this one was newer and nicer.

We found a huge room with a hardwood floor and many basketball courts, a game room with a ping pong table, and the biggest indoor swimming pool I had ever seen. I mean this pool was really big. I noticed right away that it had a regular diving board and a high dive. I had never been on a high dive before, it looked both interesting and scary at the same time.

We went to a large locker room and changed into our swimsuits. Then we all walked out to the pool with our white bodies looking pale and strange next to the bronzed bodies of the American Indian kids that were already at the pool.

We saw some parents and lots of kids at the pool. Most of the adults were women. The kids looked like they ranged from a few years to fourteen or fifteen. We wasted no time jumping into the pool and splashing around.

As I often do, after awhile I wandered off into a corner of the pool to watch everything that was going on. I saw some mothers holding their children in the water at the shallow end of the pool. Some of the little kids were afraid and others squealed with delight. I saw kids taking turns going off the low diving board. One little girl was off to the side practicing holding her breath underwater. A couple of young boys were having a good-natured wrestling match in the waist deep area of the pool. Every once in awhile someone would yell at the boys to stop; they would stop for about ten seconds, laugh, and then start again.

The high dive looked pretty tall to me. Occasionally one of the older Indian boys would jump off it, but I didn't see anyone actually dive off of it. As I watched there was a part of me that wanted to try it. There was also a part of me that didn't think it was such a good idea.

The funny thing about fear is that the more you think about it the bigger it gets, even though circumstances may not change at all. I floated in the corner with my legs sticking out toward the center of the pool. My arms were holding onto the sides and I just watched the high dive even if no one was on it, it was calling to me. The longer I stayed there the more I wanted to go off the high dive. At the same time I also became more afraid.

I tried to speak rationally to myself. Kids smaller than I had jumped off it. I was supposed to be a bit of a daredevil. What was I so afraid of?

I finally determined that I could not live with myself if I didn't take this opportunity to jump off the high dive. I simply had to do it. It didn't matter how I felt about it. This was something that just had to be done.

I had noticed that none of the other boys from camp had gone off the high dive; that made me hesitate a little. But I decided that I shouldn't live my life based on what others do or don't do, I had to decide for myself.

I figured that I may-as-well use the lower diving board a few times before I attempted the high board. I pulled myself out of the water, walked around the pool and waited my turn. There was a pretty constant stream of Indians and campers using the low board. When it was my turn I walked out to the end and bounced a few times and then I stepped back and prepared myself to dive. Taking three steps and a jump I launched myself into a front dive. It wasn't anything fancy, but I did actually know how to do a decent front dive.

I hadn't really paid much attention to who the other boys were that had come on the swimming trip. Sitting on the front seat of the van I was pretty disconnected from the group. When I stepped up to the low diving board the second time I found out that Eric Winston was one of the other boys. How I had missed his presence concerned me a little. Was I losing my touch? I always had excellent radar for these kinds of things.

It occurred to me that I was so happy and relaxed at camp that this was causing me to lose my defensive awareness. Then as I thought about it I wasn't sure if this was a good thing or a bad thing. Since I had been as happy as I had ever been in my life I decided that I didn't really care one way or the other. Eric Winston wasn't a big enough threat to me that I needed to be concerned.

Whatever the reason might be that I hadn't noticed him, I now became very aware of him. He was talking to me from in the pool as I started to climb up on the low dive and I didn't particularly like what I was hearing.

"Oh, it is the great cowboy Harry Fruitgarden!" He flavored his taunt with a sarcastic voice. "Oh, Mr. Fruitgarden is also a great diver! Yes, he is good at everything, including sitting on eggs!"

Of course he was referring to my initiation into the Royal Order of the Chicken. Only the campers would know what that meant. As I prepared to dive he started in on me being a chicken.

"Yes, Harry Fruitgarden the great chicken!" he announced to everyone who wasn't deaf at the pool.

I could instantly see every kid turn my way. Anyone who speaks English knows what being called a chicken means.

"Grow up Winston!" I yelled back in return. Then I quickly made another front dive. This one wasn't quite as good as the first, but it wasn't bad.

Coming up for air after the dive I felt pretty good. I decided that one more dive would prepare me for the high dive. I wasn't going to actually dive off the high dive; I was just going to jump, so I figured it shouldn't be too bad.

When it became my turn to dive again Eric decided to pull out all the stops.

"Ladies and Gentlemen, it is once again the great chicken Fruitgarden!" he called in a taunting voice for all to hear. Then he continued with a challenge, "Why don't you do that off the high dive Mr. Chicken Fruitgarden?" His question was followed with a classic chicken clucking sound.

For a split second I had to admire the good quality of his clucking, he was pretty good at it. That gave me an idea. "Well, Mr. Winston, you cluck so well that I think you must be a chicken yourself!" I threw back at him with no rancor in my voice.

That really made Eric mad, he hated it when I bested him verbally. The problem was that he simply didn't think quickly enough to do anything but get himself deeper into trouble, which he was about to do again.

"I challenge you!" Eric yelled out without first thinking about what he was saying .

"What challenge?" I asked immediately.

He hadn't really thought this out, he looked quickly around. Then he said with a smile, "I challenge you to dive, not jump, off the high dive."

This was a serious challenge. I hadn't seen one person dive off the high dive. And none of the boys from the Circle H Ranch had even jumped. Eric was so pleased with himself and the high quality of his challenge that he hadn't considered that I would accept it. He felt assured that I would be publicly humiliated by refusing the challenge.

I didn't hesitate for a second, I called back, "If I dive, you dive. Right?"

Eric called back with a puffed out chest and big smile, "That is right Mr. Chicken!"

"I accept," I replied instantly.

I watched my words slowly sink into Eric's apparently thick skull. He went from big grin, to what just happened?, to UhOh, what have I gotten myself into?, in a surprisingly long time.

Every kid at the pool that was over five years old was now at complete attention. All eyes were on me. No adult stepped in to stop the challenge.

I didn't even bother to take another practice dive. I climbed back down to the pool deck and walked over to the base of the high dive. I looked up and then looked at Eric. I could see hope that I wouldn't go up flicker on his face for a moment. Then as I took the first step up I looked to see his face fill with concern.

I climbed straight up the ladder without stopping. I was used to being high up on fences, so I didn't figure that aspect of the challenge would be too bad. I was wrong.

I found that once I got up on the top of the diving board the surface of the pool looked to be a mile away. It was tall, way too tall for comfort.

There was no way I was going to take steps and bounce up even higher like I had done on the low dive. So I slowly walked out toward the end. I stopped about halfway out because I was feeling a bit disoriented. I instantly knew that this was what is called vertigo. I took a couple of steps back and steadied myself by holding on to the railing next to the diving board.

Instantly Eric made another major error of judgement. He called out, "Oh yes! Mr. Chicken is chicken!"

His taunt really made me mad. Anger began to surge forth through my body and gave me the strength that I needed to overcome my fear. I knew that the longer I stood there the harder it would be so I stepped forward, looked down at Eric and called out, "You are next buddy."

Then I went right out to the end of the diving board, put my hands at my sides and started to leaned forward.

I don't really know what birds feel like when they take off from the top of a building or the side of a cliff, but I imagined that how I felt just then was pretty similar. The only difference is that birds can fly, I had to try and enter the water without killing myself.

Chapter 25

As my feet left the diving board I brought my arms up above my head and brought my hands together to make a point that I hoped would protect my head. My mind went into slow motion once again and it seemed to take forever to reach the surface of the pool. I went down and down for a long time without anything happening. I tried to angle my body for minimal impact but I was unsure about how to do it. When I arrived at the surface of the water it felt like I was like hitting a brick wall.

The good news is that I survived. That bad news is that I got a bloody nose. I came up for air with a trickle of red flowing out of my right nostril.

In a way the bloody nose was quite helpful. It didn't really hurt after the initial shock. When I saw horror reflected in Eric's face as he looked at my face I almost laughed. I didn't waste any time by being hurt, I called out to Eric with a big bloody smile, "Your turn big man!"

I could tell he was deeply afraid, so I gave him a dose of his own medicine and taunted him a bit. I didn't want him to wiggle out of this by getting an adult involved.

Then he would just say that he would have dived but the adults wouldn't let him.

The kids around the pool were pretty impressed with my bloody nose, they understood that warriors sometimes get injured. When handled with dignity, injuries were badges of honor, not of shame. That was certainly part of the Indian spirit as I understood it.

Eric wasn't particularly quick in his movements toward the high dive. Every eye was now on him. Would he chicken out of the challenge that he had proposed so brashly?

I wasn't sure which way things were going to go for awhile. Eric did make his way to the high dive and start climbing. He wasn't moving quickly, but he was moving. I tried to read his face but the only thing that I saw for sure was fear. And fear alone doesn't say if a person will or will not do something.

When Eric arrived at the top of the ladder he moved even more slowly to actually climb up onto the diving board. I heard the lone clucking of a chicken sound start to come out of a little Indian boy. I looked at the boy's face; it was a face that was simultaneously young and old. I saw a kind of confidence on his face that I wasn't used to seeing in small children. I wondered if his world made him old at a younger age then my world.

I could see that this boy was reading something besides fear in the Eric's face. Then a small chorus of boys started with the clucking sound. Eric finally heard the sound and looked around. Seeing that all of the boys in the pool, both white and dark were clucking Eric started to crumble. He was halfway down the diving board when he sat down and grabbed the side rail. He hugged the rail and closed his eyes. He was frozen.

This whole tableau was totally out of my hands now. One of the parents at the pool finally either noticed or just decided that it was time to intercede. Mysteriously, the lifeguard appeared, an Indian boy of about eighteen or nineteen. I figured that he had been watching the whole time and wanted to see what would happen. I thought that in itself was interesting.

It took some time, but Eric was eventually coaxed off the high dive and down the ladder. He was taken right into the locker room. Strangely I think it ended up being a good experience for him. After that he never bothered me or anyone that I know again. In a way I felt sorry for him. I never really disliked him, I just didn't see why I should put up with his attitude. Exactly what he went through I don't know, but I do know that I was glad to have him off my back.

Once the excitement was over I cleaned my face up at a drinking fountain and swam around some more. My display of courage seemed to have a positive affect on the Indian boys in the pool. Several of them came up to me and smiled.

One boy actually said, "You are brave." I didn't know how to respond to that so I just smiled at him.

When the skin on my fingers and toes was nice and wrinkled I decided that I had spent enough time in the pool. I changed back into my boots, jeans and hat. Then I decided that the next order of business was to take a private tour of the facility.

I checked out the big room were some Indian boys were playing basketball. Then I went into the little game room. There I found two of the camp boys playing ping-pong. I watched for awhile and then left to continue my tour.

I wandered down a hall and found a room with soda and candy dispensers. There was an old Indian man sitting at a table. When I walked in I looked at him and he looked at me. I didn't want to disturb him so I started to leave, but he called to me.

"Come," he said in a voice that was both commanding and gentle. "Come, sit down." He pointed with his finger at me and motioned for me to sit.

As I walked over to the table and sat across from the old man I inspected his wrinkled face. His eyes were clear and he looked at me closely, just as I looked at him. His hair was long and pulled back in a braid. There was a feather sticking out of his hair at the top of the braid.

This was a real Indian elder like I had seen in movies, yet he lived today. I was fascinated. We sat there looking at each other for a few moments. He didn't seem to mind that I was inspecting him. He wasn't shy about inspecting me. I was fascinated by the way he looked and the history that he represented.

Then he said, "What is your name Little Man?

"My name is Harry Fruitgarden," I answered.

"That is an unusual name," he commented. Then he lapsed into silence. I got the impression that he was thinking about something. I couldn't even begin to fathom what it might be.

I asked, "Why did you call me Little Man?"

"You were brave on the diving board," he responded.

"You saw what happened?" I asked.

The old man nodded a yes and continued to look at me with penetrating eyes.

"What is your name?" I asked.

"I am called Resting Eagle," he replied. "I am also called Bob."

That made me laugh and then he laughed. In that shared moment we seemed to find an instant bond.

When we were done smiling he looked again at me, or maybe through me, it was hard to tell. Then Resting Eagle said. "You have had dreams?"

I was shocked by his question. No one in the world knew of my dreams. How could he have known? My shock seemed to confirm his suspicions. He nodded that he understood my surprise. He then asked, "Have you seen the ancestors?"

Once again he seemed to read my face without me needing to answer verbally. It seemed silly to acknowledge what he already knew to be true so I asked, "How do you know these things?"

"Who can say how it is that water is wet?" Resting Eagle said, "It just is. That is its nature."

His answer sounded pretty cool, but it didn't really explain anything in a way that I could fully understand. When he saw the frustration in my eyes Resting Eagle said, "You are young and impatient. As you grow you will find that silence speaks louder than sounds. Don't let your mind understand only science. Oh, science isn't bad, but it is not everything. Look also for that which you will find beyond science, in silence and in nature"

"Who did I see in my dreams?" I asked.

"What did you see?" he asked as an answer.

"First I saw a white horse. It led me to a group of people sitting around a fire. There was an old man. I think he saw me. I dreamed this at Mesa Verde." I answered.

"That is a good dream. You have been invited to know more about the source that gives life to the world that we see with our eyes," Resting Eagle said.

We sat in silence for a minute or two. I wondered if all of this was real.

"You are favored by the Great Spirit," Resting Eagle said nodding his head. "This is good but you must educate yourself in these things if you want to understand them more."

"How do I do that?" I asked.

"Keep your eyes open for opportunities to learn. Don't doubt that there is something to learn. If you believe that you can learn, you will," Resting Eagle said with confidence. He went on to say, "Many people do not believe in things that the senses can not reach. But if you follow your heart you will know what is true and what is not true."

"Are all American Indians wise?" I asked.

My question made Resting Eagle laugh. "You have been watching too many movies Little Man," he said. "Men and women are not wise because of the color of their skin, the language that they speak or the place on earth that they live. Wisdom, peace and love come from the Great Spirit. Those from any time and place who know the Great Spirit are wise. Those who do not are wandering thirsty in a desert."

After another pause Resting Eagle gave me one more bit of advice, "Do not be in a hurry to finish being a boy, Little Man. The world of grownups will be upon you soon enough by itself."

We sat there for a few minutes in silence, I pondering what Resting Eagle said and He doing I don't know what. He just sat there with a little smile on his face. I was just about to stand up and go when Resting Eagle stood, reached up and pulled the feather from his hair. He then reached out toward me and offered me the feather.

"This eagle feather has been in my family for many generations," Resting Eagle said. "It has been passed from father to son many times. The Great Spirit has not given me a son to pass it to. If you will allow me, I will pass it to you."

I didn't know what to say. This turn of events was so out of the realm of my life. Here I was being given a gift that held a value to this man higher than a mountain of gold. I didn't see any way that I could be worthy of such a gift. I also didn't see any way I could refuse it.

I looked at Resting Eagle and saw in has face that if I rejected this gift I would be rejecting him and his desire to fulfill his part of the ancestral chain. I stood up, reached out and accepted the sacred feather.

Finding words that I didn't know were within me I said, "I am deeply honored Resting Eagle. I will do my best to pass this on as you have done."

As the feather passed from his hand to mine I felt a kind of tingle go up my arms and flood my body with love and good feeling. It was strange and wonderful at the same time.

Resting Eagle smiled. I could see that this had pleased him very much. Placing the feather in my hat I resolved to put it in a safer place once I got back to camp.

Then Resting Eagle surprised me with an announcement. "Now that this is taken care of," he said with a smile, "It is time to eat. What kind of candy do you like?"

We then spent the next thirty minutes eating candy and discussing the merits and disadvantages of the various kinds of candy. By the time we were done I was full of sugar and felt like I had been visiting with as good a friend as I had ever had. Resting Eagle had become a child in an old body. There was nothing hidden or strange about our conversation. It was just plain fun.

When it became time for me to go I didn't hesitate to give Resting Eagle a hug. I had never known my grandfather on either my father's or my mother's side of the family. I embraced Resting Eagle as my grandfather and I believe he felt towards me as if I were a grandson.

As our group later rode back to camp in the van I was once again filled with how strange life can be. If I hadn't gotten into trouble for taking the horse when I knew it was the wrong thing to do, so many good things wouldn't have happened. I simply didn't know what to think about the way life works, but I did marvel at the way life works.

Chapter 26

After the day that I went to the Reservation I got back into my routine of riding almost every day. Often at the end of the day I would pull out the eagle feather that Resting Eagle had given me and think of him. Then I would put it away in the bottom of my suitcase where I was confident that no one would find it.

Some time during the fifth week of camp Ken approached me to go out on a ride with just the two of us. We decided to go bareback. He would ride Lady and I would ride Sparky. I had ridden bareback a number of times, but not for any great distance. This would be a test of my bareback stamina.

We headed out late in the morning on a day when most of the campers had gone away on a day trip in the vans. We packed some food since there was little chance we would be back in time for dinner (lunch).

As we left camp the sky was clear, the sun was hot, and our anticipation of a carefree day was high. We walked our horses for the first half-mile and then set them to a comfortable cantor. The horses started to cover some ground, but they were in good shape so they didn't get overly winded.

The farther we went the more I relaxed into the rhythm of Sparky's gait. She was very smooth when she cantered like this. Riding bareback I could feel totally connected to her muscles. She felt like a steel coil that was just being loosened a little. I could tell that she was completely comfortable and could maintain this pace for some time.

As we made our way down the trail I held only to the reins. If we went through a patch of ground that was a little rough I would grab a handful of hair at the base of Sparky's mane as a hand hold. My hat was firmly placed on my head so I couldn't feel the wind in my hair, but my face was invigorated by the flow of air as we made our way across an open meadow.

We walked the horses across a stream and squeezed our legs tight to stay in position as we rode up the steep opposite bank. After riding for about an hour and a half at various paces we stopped by a stream that was about six feet wide. We let the horses drink deeply from the clear fresh water and let them graze on the nearby grass. They were as happy as can be.

We explored the general area and talked a little about our lives away from camp. Ken's family was from Mesa, Arizona. I had never seen his whole family all at once so it was new information to learn that Ken had four sisters and four brothers. I couldn't imagine what it would be like to have such a large family.

When I told him a few stories from my life in California it seemed far away and remote - like someone other than me had actually had those experiences.

We drank fresh water from the stream and then we took our boots off and soaked our feet in the refreshing water. We broke off long stems of grass from the meadow and chewed on them as we talked. As Ken described his years of horse experience I was both educated and amazed that he had done so much with horses. I hadn't realized that he actually owned three horses of his own. The third horse was back where he lived in Arizona.

As we wandered and talked we failed to notice that the sky had become gray. In the middle of a discussion on the merits of a straight bit versus a snaffle bit we were interrupted by a flash of lightning followed quickly by a very loud clap of thunder. The thunder was so loud that we instinctively flinched in reaction. I had never been so closed to thunder this loud, it was a little scary.

Ken immediately walked towards where we had last seen the horses. They weren't there. We looked around but found that we couldn't find them. Ken hypothesized that the thunder had spooked them and that they had run off, probably towards camp.

We didn't have much time to ponder where they were because large drops of rain began to fall. Then there was another flash of lightning that was frighteningly close, followed almost immediately with an even louder clap of thunder than the first one - which had already been too loud for comfort.

"Let's go Harry," Ken directed as he started to walk.

As I turned to follow I asked, "Where we going?"

"I'll show you," was the only answer I could get from Ken.

By the time we got to the edge of the meadow rain was coming down pretty hard. Since we had been riding bareback we didn't have any way to bring ponchos, we were going to get soaked.

I noticed right away that Ken didn't seem to be bothered by any of this. His calm kept me from dwelling on thoughts like: we are about to get soaked by the rain and then fried by lightning and then if we aren't completely dead we are going to have to walk home in the dark!

I was once again reminded by the intensity of the elements that I was a city boy playing at being a country boy. I had never lived close to the power of nature. Lightning and thunder from a distance is cool, being right up next to it in the mountains with no protection is frightening. The closest I had ever been to lightning in the past was when I could count to four or five after I saw the flash, before the sound of thunder arrived. We were now experiencing lightning and thunder almost simultaneously. It was close - very close.

I almost bumped into Ken when we got to the edge of the meadow. He had stopped and was looking around at the trees. He apparently was trying to make a decision of some kind. It didn't take him long.

"This way Harry," Ken said.

I followed close behind Ken. The raindrops were coming down hard now. We walked along the edge of the meadow until we arrived at the spot that Ken felt was right. We then scurried in under a medium sized pine tree that had particularly thick branches. I was amazed to find that when we got in under the tree and sat down the ground was dry. The tree was acting like a big umbrella.

Ken said, "I chose this one because it has lots of thick branches. Also, it isn't one of the tallest trees; that will lessen the chance of it being struck by ...."

Ken's words were cut off by the closest flash of lightning and the loudest crack of thunder we had yet experienced. It was both frightening and exhilarating at the same time. I felt like we weren't just near the storm, but we were up in it. The power and immensity of the forces being displayed by nature were awesome.

We had a perfect view from under our tree. We could see out across the meadow to the forested slope on the other side. The meadow was maybe fifty yards across. The rain was coming down hard now but we were dry under our tree.

The dark, almost black, clouds were bumping and crashing into each other right before our eyes. There were rumbles of thunder constantly. Every few moments lightning would flash and we would hear a cracking sound that would not only assault our ears but go right down deep into our bones.

The storm continued to build for about twenty minutes. We just sat quietly under our tree and watched the show. It was like nothing I would ever have believed if someone had tried to tell me about it. We felt hidden and protected under our tree, but I also knew that things could change. I just didn't realize how right I was.

There was a point at which it appeared that the storm was abating slightly. I remember having the thought that maybe the worst was over. Just a few moments later we instinctively covered our eyes and ears as a bolt of lighting struck a tree not more than one hundred feet from us. It was as if a bomb had exploded.

Fortunately the tree that got hit was to the side of us. We weren't actually looking at it when the top half of the tree exploded. It was so loud and bright that our bodies took control and tried to protect themselves. We rolled over on our sides and covered our heads with our arms.

The thing that I remember so clearly was a strange electric stirring in the air just as the lightning hit the tree. Then there was an odor in the air that I will always associate with lighting. The top of the tree was completely blown off and the bottom of the tree was burning even though the rain was trying to put out the flames.

There is no question that we were both scared out of our wits. We huddled under our tree with our arms wrapped around our knees and hoped for the best. We knew we had to stay put. I had a brief thought that I hoped the horses were okay, more than that I was unable to manage. This had gone way beyond exciting and well into the terrifying category.

The storm lasted for about an hour. I was amazed that even though it rained hard, we were perfectly dry under the tree that Ken had chosen. We stayed under the tree until we were sure it was safe. Patches of blue sky started to appear and after awhile the sun once again established its presence in the sky.

The earth was dark and wet. The grass was a deep rich green. The forest started to come alive again with the sounds of birds. We saw a deer peek its head out of the forest and nibble on some grass in the meadow. This was nature at its freshest.

I had always thought of nature as being benign and friendly. Living in harmony with nature seemed like a walk in the park. The forces of nature that we saw displayed that day were so powerful that I had to rethink my understanding of nature. Nature had many facets that I would need to explore more fully in order to understand how all of life fit together.

"Well, we may as well get going," Ken said starting to walk in the direction of camp.

"We are going to walk back to camp?" I asked.

"Have you got a better idea?" Ken asked in return.

I couldn't think of one, so I started walking. We set a steady pace, not fast, but not plodding. We weren't sure how long it was going to take to get back, so we figured that we should not wear ourselves out by walking too quickly in the beginning.

We walked for a long time. As we rounded each new bend in the trail we searched in vain for signs of Lady and Sparky. Our conversation ebbed and flowed like a breeze that can't decide if it wants to blow. Even though I enjoyed talking to Ken, I also liked that we didn't need to talk all of the time. I had always found that silence gave me time to sort out my many thoughts and feelings.

It seemed like we walked for a long, long time. My legs started to get weary, but I didn't say anything. I was quite relieved that when we arrived at the capture the flag meadow we found Lady and Sparky munching on grass as if they didn't have a care in the world. They were both uninjured. Even though their backs were wet from the rain we mounted up and headed back to camp.

Just as we arrived we met Maurice heading our way on a horse. "So I see you guys haven't been fried to a crisp!" Maurice said in greeting.

"Nah," Ken responded as if we had been caught in a light sprinkle. "We just crawled in under a tree and hunkered down for awhile."

"Well, your mother was a little concerned about you two and asked me to see if I could find you," Maurice informed us.

Ken nodded that he understood. "We'll go say hello to her so she knows we are okay," Ken said.

Maurice then turned his horse and headed back to the tack house. We went to find Mrs. Hutchins. We found her all a flutter about our safety. But she calmed down pretty quickly when she saw that we weren't injured. She asked about me as well as Ken. I appreciated that.

By the time that we arrived back at the tack house it was time to feed the horses. After taking the bridles off Lady and Sparky we released them into the corral. When we were done feeding the horses we headed back to the lodge for supper.

While we ate supper we heard many of the boys talking about the storm. They had been in the vans driving down the road when it hit the area they were in. It had rained hard and they had seen some lightning but they hadn't been out in it the way we had. Ken and I smiled at each other. I couldn't help thinking as I put a big mouthful of mashed potatoes into my mouth, that it was good to be alive!

Chapter 27

I found that thinking I might die caused me to remember the important people in my life. I wondered what my family had been doing while I was away at camp. I couldn't help wishing that we were a close family like Ken's. That made me wonder how it is that some families are close and some are not? Which led to the question: Could a family that wasn't close become close?

I felt certain that Resting Eagle would have some valuable thoughts to share on this subject, but it seemed unlikely that I would see him again. I tried to imagine what he might say, but I couldn't think of a poetic way to express my ideas. I was pretty convinced that anything Resting Eagle said on a serious subject would be poetic!

It occurred to me that when a tree grows crooked you can tie it in such a way as to cause it to grow straight. I had seen a gardener do that at our house once. I wasn't sure how you could tie a family. The idea that you could apply some energy to make things better did make sense.

I also thought a lot about Shannon. As the summer progressed we had managed to spend some time together here and there. Not as much time as I would have liked, but enough that we continued to feel closer as friends instead of farther apart.

I had helped her wash dishes a few more times. We had walked in the moonlight one night during the evening program - as far as I knew no one had noticed. One afternoon we went on a walk and spent a couple of hours by the river.

When I went to the river with Shannon that day I discovered something that I had never quite understood about girls: Girls are just people. I know that might seem like an obvious and silly thing to have figured out, but the truth is that during the last year I had noticed that the more I observed girls and wanted to talk with them, the less I knew about them. And the idea of spending any length of time with a girl had seemed pretty much impossible.

The first problem is that asking a girl to spend time with you is like trying to talk with peanut butter in your mouth, the words just can't come out. Why this should be is a mystery to me...but I had observed it in other boys and experienced it myself. Then if you manage to get past that stage you have to figure out what you want the girl to do with you. You can't ask a girl to spend time with you while you build a fort or climb a tree. You have to ask a girl to do something that she will want to do. And we all know that the thing girls most like to do is talk.

Now talking can be good. But it can also be difficult when you feel affected in the brain by being in the presence of a girl that causes your brain not to function too clearly.

What I found with Shannon is that when I was doing something like helping her clean the dishes or walking somewhere, those simple tasks allowed me to calm myself and gradually feel relaxed and comfortable. Once that happened I discovered that girls like to have adventures to, depending on their interests.

Shannon liked to throw rocks, look for pollywogs, and tell funny stories that had happened to her or others that she knew. She apparently enjoyed listening to me as well. She would ask a question and then I would speak eloquently until I had nothing more to say. If my thoughts bored her she covered it up really well. I checked regularly to see if she was listening and she was; that made me feel good. I wasn't used to people wanting to hear what I had to say.

I found that it didn't really matter what we talked about, it just mattered that we were enjoying our time spent together. Once I got past the initial shock of spending time with her I felt quite comfortable. I could even not talk for awhile and it was okay. She seemed to understand silence as well as conversation.

On days that we didn't get to spend any time together I noticed that if I saw her during the day and she looked at me and smiled or winked, the whole rest of my day was brighter. She just had that kind of affect on me.

We never talked about how we felt about each other. I'm not really sure why. Maybe we didn't talk about it because we couldn't define it or describe it exactly. I do know that it was very special to me. Maybe it was one of those things in life that gets lessened when it is no longer private.

I also spent time during the summer looking for special thinking spots. One place I liked to disappear to was on top of the haystack. All of the bales of hay that we would feed the horses were stacked ten or twelve feet high. I would climb up to the top and find a place in the middle where I couldn't be seen. There I would pull a piece of the hay out from one of the bales and munch on it as I lounged on top of the little hay mountain.

The hay smelled fresh and fragrant. It was comfortable to lay on and no one would see me up there if I didn't want them too. One time I heard a couple of adults arguing with each other. They obviously didn't know I was around. I felt like I was eavesdropping on a private conversation but once they had started I didn't want to reveal myself.

I wasn't really interested in what they were arguing about, but it did occur to me that they were both unclear about what they should do concerning whatever it was they were talking about. Their discussion made me think about being an adult. I thought that adults were supposed to know how life works and what to do in any situation. What good does it do to grow up if you still don't know what to do with yourself? Then it occurred to me that maybe growing older and growing up weren't the same thing.

Another place that I liked to visit was a small corral that was hidden by some trees in the back corner of the larger corral that all of the horses stayed in at night. I would walk over there sometimes and find a horse that was being kept separate from the larger group. Usually it was because it was a new horse that wasn't yet ready to ride. Occasionally it was a horse that had been injured and needed some time alone and special care.

I would spend time talking to those horses when I could. I figured they must be a bit lonely all by themselves, away from the herd. So I would bring an apple or a carrot and feed them while I talked and patted their necks. Some of the horses were nervous at first. Over time I found that all of them would come to me eventually if I was patient enough. It always felt good when a horse that hesitated to come over to me finally accepted me and became friendly.

One day I found a horse in there that was really wild. As soon as I arrived it headed for the opposite end of the corral. I went back every day for a week and brought it an apple. The only way I could get the horse to eat the apple was to throw it across to him. He would then eat it off the ground.

It seemed like the more the horse didn't want to be near me, the more I wanted to be near it. By the end of the second week I finally got the horse to take the apple out of my hand. After that I would pat its neck while it nibbled on the apple.

One day Ken found me out there and saw that I was patting the horses neck. He was amazed. He told me that one of his brothers had been trying to do the same thing with no luck. At the time I didn't think much of it, but a few days later Shannon told me that Ken had mentioned it to their Dad. Shannon said that they had all been surprised and impressed.

There was one other place that I liked to go when I had enough time. I never told others I went because I thought that maybe I wasn't supposed to go. I would walk up the driveway to the main road and cross the street. On the other side of the road was a steep hillside that I would climb until I could look down on the Circle H Ranch from above. I liked being up where I could see the overview of the whole place. I would watch people go about their day and wonder what they were thinking. It reminded me a little of being on my roof at home and watching the neighborhood.

I didn't feel like a spy up there, I wasn't trying to invade anyone's privacy. I was just observing life from a distance. I found going up there allowed me to see things and get ideas that I wouldn't get if I was right down in the middle of everything. It was a bird's eye view. My thoughts and imagination would soar like an eagle from up there.

One day I saw Maurice bringing the horses down from the far meadow just as Ken had done the day I arrived at camp. The horses didn't run wild like they had that first day. Maurice was riding a horse called Jumper. Only Maurice was allowed to ride that horse. It was a beautiful horse: tall and strong. Jumper was a rich dark brown with particularly shiny coat. The shiny coat made him seem to shimmer.

One day Ken had told me the story about Jumper. Ken said, "We got Jumper from the auction about three months ago. He was really wild when he arrived. He got his name Jumper because he would jump out of every corral he was put in. We finally had to put another rail up on the inner corral so that we could keep him in one place. Maurice got tossed off him plenty of times before he finally stayed on."

I couldn't help wishing I had seen some of those sessions. I could tell even from my short experience that Jumper was a special horse.

As I watched Maurice ride I noticed how comfortable he looked. He just seemed to be a part of the horse. I was admiring his riding style when they were walking past the lodge and a camper leaving the lodge allowed the screen door on the front porch to slam. It became instantly apparent that Jumper didn't like the noise.

Since I happened to be watching Maurice when this happened I got to see the whole thing. As soon as the door made the noise Jumper did just that, he jumped. All four legs leapt surprisingly far straight up in the air. At the same time he lowered his head, which is essential for horses to do when they want to buck, and went at trying to toss Maurice off like they were at the National Finals Rodeo.

The thing that amazed me was that Maurice just flowed with it like it was an everyday occurrence. He did grab the saddle horn with his right hand while holding the reins in his left, but he didn't seem to be trying to stop the event in any way, and he stayed put in the saddle. When Jumper was done and Maurice was still in the saddle they proceeded to walk toward the corral as if nothing had taken place. It amazed me.

I knew instantly that I had a lot to learn about riding. At the same time, I felt good about being able to recognize what a good rider looked like. I also felt good that I was moving in the direction of becoming a good rider. I determined to increase my efforts at improving my riding skills.

Chapter 28

As one summer day melted into another I completely lost track of time. I had neither calendar nor watch to tell me the day or hour. Only the movement of the sun across the sky gave me a sense of where I was in the current day. The world outside camp receded far from my mind and the weeks flew by. I was happier and more carefree than I had ever been.

Life at camp was paradise to me. I couldn't even imagine anything more perfect. So when a large group of us saddled up for a three-day and two-night trip up into the high country, I had no idea that life was to reach whole new levels of perfection and depression.

The culmination of each group's experience at the Circle H Ranch was a camping trip on horseback. I had been on several of these trips during the summer and they were glorious. This was to be the final trip of the summer, three days and two nights out on the trail in God's Country. We would load up the horses with saddlebags filled with food, tie on our sleeping bags and then head out into the wilderness of the San Juan Mountains.

Maurice, Ken, Mr. Williams, Jonesy and Mr. Davis were all coming on this trip. There were forty-five riders including myself. Ken and I prepared ourselves to take up our positions at the rear of the line. With this many riders the group would get stretched out quite a bit. We would be in charge of helping any of the boys that had trouble keeping up or had a problem of any kind.

As the group left camp everyone was in great spirits. Mr. and Mrs. Hutchins and several others of the camp staff stood on the porch of the lodge to give us a good send off. I couldn't help thinking that they were probably thinking about how nice it was going to be with camp empty for a few days. It was a little disappointing when I looked for Shannon and didn't see her; I had hoped she would appear for the send off.

Ken and I were still standing on the ground as we helped some of the boys get up on their horses. It was a lot harder to mount when you had to get your right leg up and over a sleeping bag and saddlebags. Several of the boys had to place their horses next to the porch of the lodge and sort of slide down onto the saddle. We had seen this before and it was a pretty funny sight, but quite practical. Although, there was little chance these boys were going to find a porch to help them the next time they needed to get on or off their horse. I inwardly smiled as I thought about the coming adventures while I watched the long line form and start in a snake-like motion to head out of camp.

Just as I was about to mount Sparky, Shannon came running up to me. Most of the group had left so it was a less dramatic moment than it might have been - which was fine with me. She handed me a little package, smiled and executed one of her patented sprightly exits before I had a chance to say anything.

I put the package in my saddlebags under Ken's smirking gaze and mounted my horse. I figured the pleasure of Shannon's friendship was worth a little ribbing so I didn't say anything. Since we were slightly delayed from the rest of the group we trotted our horses to catch up.

Once the group got out onto the trail everything went smoothly for the first couple of hours. I found that sitting in the saddle and rocking to the motion of Sparky's walk was soothing to my mind. Sometimes I would think about a specific subject, like Shannon or Resting Eagle. At other times I would let my mind wander to seek its own sense of harmony. I would mentally reach out into the forest or up into the sky. I found that just being out in nature and trying to feel its life was both comforting and inspiring.

The first bump in our trip was when one of the newer boys decided that he had to use nature's bathroom - otherwise known as the bushes. Ken and I didn't see what actually happened but we did see the results. In order to facilitate his need he just hopped off his horse and headed for the bushes to take care of business. His horse, a bay gelding named, Socks, because it had three white ankles, decided that it wanted to keep its place in line so it just kept going without its rider.

When the boy was done in the bushes he ran up alongside the line and caught up to his horse. Unfortunately he made a cardinal mistake. All new riders are warned not to run up behind a horse without announcing yourself. This boy forgot to do so and paid the price.

The first indication that there was a problem was when Ken and I heard a boy scream. We jumped off our horses and ran up to the scene of the difficulty. While we scrambled through the forest to get around all the horses in front of us we couldn't imagine what the problem could be. Arriving at the scene we found a boy lying on his back, having trouble breathing. It didn't take us long to figure out what had happened. When we lifted up the boy's shirt we found the impression of a horse's shoe on the skin of his stomach.

Ken told the boy to try and take slow deep breaths. I asked one of the boys nearby to tell us what happened. Our deduction was correct. The boy had run up behind his horse, which had spooked the horse and caused it to kick out in reflex.

Soon Jonesy, Mr. Davis and Mr. Williams arrived and took over the boy's care. It appeared the boy wasn't seriously hurt, but all three adults agreed that the boy should be taken back to camp just in case he exhibited new symptoms over time. Mr. Davis volunteered to take the boy back to camp.

Along with my concern for the boy I couldn't help thinking that I didn't like the idea that Mr. Davis was going back. I didn't fully trust Mr. Williams to behave himself. Even though we had smoothed things over during the summer, I had the feeling there was still some bad blood boiling deep inside his mind and I didn't want to be the recipient of his anger when those feelings came to the surface. I figured that Jonesy, Maurice and Ken were allies enough, but I knew that Mr. Davis was the strongest way to keep Mr. Williams in check.

My misgivings didn't last long. I decided that even if there was something to be concerned about, it was too late to do anything about it. Had I known what was going to happen I might have gone back to camp with Mr. Davis, but that is what makes the future… the future – we don't yet know exactly what is going to happen. Soon we were back on the trail heading toward the high pastures and eventually the tree line, where even the stoutest tree can no longer grow.

The rest of the day kept us busy with little events but no major incidents. One boy got a bruise on his knee when his horse passed a tree too closely. Another boy fell into a small creek when we stopped for a drink of the cool mountain water. There was one fellow who always needed help getting on and off his horse. One time he was determined to get off himself and he fell the last couple of feet: nothing injured except his pride.

At dinnertime we stopped for peanut butter and jelly sandwiches. The horses grazed in a small meadow while we soaked our feet in a four-foot wide creek. We made sure to tell all the boys to drink their water from upstream of the foot bathers!

By late afternoon we found ourselves in a large open meadow surrounded by trees and mountain slopes with steep sides. There was small clear stream to provide water. Jonesy decided that this was a good place to camp for the night. Maurice, Ken and I helped all of the boys get their sleeping bags and saddle bags off the horses. Then we unsaddled all of the horses and let them graze in the meadow for their supper.

While the wranglers took care of the horses all of the boys were sent out to collect firewood. Soon there was a large pile of sticks and logs, that had been scattered by nature on the forest floor, sitting next to our new open air kitchen. Jonesy found some large rocks and set them at the right distance so three iron skillets could be placed over them for cooking.

By the time we were done with the horses the edge of the meadow was littered with open sleeping bags and the smell of food was wafting on the cooling late afternoon breeze. Ken and I set about building a little tent with our rain ponchos. We had done this before on campouts. Sometimes boys laughed at us for taking time to make our tent, but when we appeared with dry clothes in the morning after evening showers they were always contrite and ended up asking us how to make their own tent for the next night.

Ken seemed to know with some kind of sixth sense if it was going to rain at night. If he indicated we should build the tent, I knew it was going to rain. If he didn't say anything about a tent I knew it wouldn't rain. On clear nights we would just lay our ponchos on the grass and gaze up at the night sky that was filled with a brightness that needed no flashlight.

I tried to predict what Ken would say about the weather for that night, but I never figured out what the signals were that he was reading. Sometimes it was cloudy in the late afternoon and we wouldn't build a tent. Sometimes it was clear and we would build the tent. Like I said, he had some kind of sixth sense about knowing what the weather would do. When I asked Ken how he knew, he just shrugged his shoulders without saying a word.

This tendency to take his talents as nothing to be excited about was something that I admired about Ken. He was very knowledgeable about nature and the ways of horses, but he never acted superior about it. Most of the guys that I knew from school were always talking about how great they were at sports. They wanted to be acknowledged and looked up to for their accomplishments. Ken always acted like it was no big deal that he knew what he knew.

Ken's attitude made me think about what kind of person I was. I certainly liked it when I was praised for being good at something. But I had noticed that praise is short lived and people are often quick to turn against those who have been praised, just to bring them down a notch. It seemed to me that the important part of this was how I felt as a person and not how others treated me. Being too full of myself separated me from others, while being humble helped me to be closer to others. It struck me that this wasn't a simple issue.

When I thought about humility I remembered my pact with God to be good. I also remembered Resting Eagle. I knew that he was a very wise man, but he didn't act all stuck up with his understanding. He seemed more like a nice old guy that you wouldn't suspect was so wise unless you took the time to get to know him. He was just the opposite of the guy who gets a touchdown in football and prances around like he was the greatest thing since pancakes.

Speaking of pancakes, it was pancakes that started to bring Mr. William's bad feelings towards me back to the surface, but I didn't know that as the sun set on our first night out from camp. Thinking about pancakes reminded me that I was hungry and that supper was probably just about ready to be eaten. There is something about food that is cooked over an open fire that just makes it taste better. I don't know exactly what it is, but when you are out on the trail and you cook any kind of food, it will taste the best it has ever tasted, even if you burn it a little. This was another mystery that I wish someone would explain to me. Although, I was happy it was true even if I didn't know why it was true.

Jonesy and Mr. Williams cooked with amazing efficiency considering we were out in the middle of nowhere. For supper we had all the burgers and potato chips we could eat. For desert we opened large tins of sliced peaches. I had never considered fruit as a desert before, but out on the trail the cool sweet syrupy peaches were an absolute delight. All and all, it was not a bad meal for a group of weary horsemen.

Just before dark Maurice, Ken and I headed out to tie up the horses for the night. Each horse was tied with a rope high enough up a tree so that they couldn't step over the rope and get into trouble during the night. We had to make sure the horses were close enough to each other to feel companionship but far enough away that they couldn't kick each other.

It was fully dark when we arrived back at the campfire. Large logs had been thrown on the flames so that all of the boys could feel the heat as we surrounded the fire. Once everyone was settled Jonesy began to tell us the story of the Wild Woman of Squaw Creek. I had heard the story before, but most of the boys had not.

Chapter 29

As every good storyteller can, Jonesy wove his tale with colorful animation. He would use both a loud and soft voice. He would sit up straight at times and slump at others. His hands painted pictures in the air as sparks from the fire rose high up into the sky. We were all taken in by the tone and cadence of Jonesy's voice, along with the quiet horror of the story.

It seems that some hundred years ago or so there was a woman who lived maybe twenty or thirty miles from where we were camping. She had lived with her husband and two children, a boy and a girl. In those days neighbors were far and few between, each family was pretty much on its own to survive in the wilderness. In order to get supplies that they couldn't provide on their own they would grow food that they could take to barter with in a small town about twelve miles away.

One day the woman took the buckboard to town with a large supply of vegetables that she had grown. Why her husband didn't go with her is another part of the mystery that no one can explain. In any case, after her long trip to town and back she arrived late in the day back at the cabin to find it empty. Her husband and children were gone. There was no sign of a struggle and nothing was taken from the cabin.

The next day, after a frantic and sleepless night of calling in the forest for her husband and children, the woman rode back into town to see if her family was somehow in town. She searched all over asking everyone she saw if they had seen her family. Soon the word spread and several people offered to ride back to her cabin with her to try and figure out what had happened.

Over the next few weeks the woman found much support from the town's folk. Everyone was very concerned about what had happened, but no explanation for the disappearance could be found.

As the days turned to weeks and then months, the woman gradually started to deteriorate. She stopped coming to town very often. When she did come to town people could see by her haggard appearance that she was not taking care of herself. Her hair was not combed and her clothes were dirty, torn and tattered.

People tried to help her, but she became more and more withdrawn. She spent most of every day and night riding around the valleys near her cabin and calling for her family. It was a terrible situation but no one knew what to do.

One day when she did come to town the woman came up behind a child and grabbed the poor boy by the shoulders calling out in a frightful voice, "Are you my child?"

She scared the child half to death. And when she started doing this on a regular basis people knew that she had gone crazy with grief. Every once in a while she would find another child and cry out, "Are you my child?"

This scared both the children and the parents. Soon everyone kept their distance from the woman who had now received the name, Wild Woman from Squaw Creek.

The Wild Woman rode the trails of mountain and meadow night and day. People said that she would sometimes be seen by the light of the full moon, riding through the night and calling out for her family.

No one ever knew what happened to the Wild Woman of Squaw Creek and her family. The town's folk just noticed over a period of months that she never came to town again. Once a couple of brave men went to her cabin but didn't find her.

Everyone just assumed that she had died out on the trail looking for her family. As the years passed and the town grew, more people traveled in the area during the day and night. Every once in awhile someone would come back to town reporting that they had seen a wild looking woman riding through the dark in a storm. They thought she was yelling for something but couldn't quite understand what it was.

Sightings of the Wild Woman of Squaw Creek went on for so many years that many thought that it was her ghost wandering the hills in anguish over her loss. To this day people still say that she wanders at night looking for her children.

Jonesy ended his story with a warning that all of us should be careful as we went back to our sleeping bags. We should all keep an eye out for the Wild Woman of Squaw Creek lest she sneak up behind us and ask us, "Are you my child?"

When Jonesy said these last words he raised his voice and a couple of boys twitched in surprise. Then everyone laughed. We all rested in the knowledge that this was just a story. Silence settled over the group for a few moments and then from the darkness behind us we heard a voice yell out frightfully, "Are you my child?"

216

Then one of the boys farthest from the fire felt two hands take hold of his shoulders from the back. He instantly jumped up from his seat like a Jack in the Box and screamed at the top of his lungs. His fear was so sincere that half the group jumped up and started to move away from the poor boy.

When Mr. Williams stepped forward so his face could be seen in the firelight, most of the boys broke into the comfort of laughter. The boy who had screamed took a moment to get over his shock, but soon he too was laughing in relief. It had been a perfect double ending.

After that the campfire broke up, boys headed off to their sleeping bags to get much needed rest after a long day on the trail. The sky was clear as Ken and I tucked ourselves into our little tent. I wondered if this would be the night that Ken was wrong about us needing to build it.

Ken and I talked for awhile about the day's events. We both agreed that the imprint of the horse's shoe on that boy's stomach was amazingly clear, we hoped the boy was okay. And even though we had both heard the story of the Wild Woman of Squaw Creek before, we agreed that it had gone off tonight with particularly good effect.

We discussed the merits of sneaking up on a couple of boys to scare them now that everyone was tucked in for the night, but we decided that we were too comfortable to get out of our warm sleeping bags. Then our conversation wandered in no particular direction until we started to get sleepy. As we started to doze off I took one last look out of the end of our tent and saw the edge of a cloud cover some of the stars in the sky.

Some time in the middle of the night I awoke to the sound of raindrops hitting our tent. I couldn't help smiling at the thought that Ken's weather guessing streak was still at 100 percent. I took a short moment to feel sorry for the boys who hadn't prepared for rain and then snuggled deeper into my sleeping bag.

Chapter 30

When we rose early in the morning the sky was once again clear. The meadow grass was wet from the late night rain; I was glad that I had kept the grease coating on my boots in good shape. Ken and I set out to untie the horses so they could eat their moist green breakfast. By the time we got to the morning fire there were about fifteen boys huddled closely around the warmth. They were wet, cold and a bit grumpy.

I suppose it wasn't very kind of me, but when Mr. Williams arrived wet and cold I couldn't help smiling. I did at least turn my head so that he couldn't see my face. That was a wise thing to do because the first boy that got between him and the fire got yelled at. Apparently he was more than a bit grumpy this morning.

For some reason I was feeling particularly chipper that morning. I felt like all was good with the world and I wasn't going to let some cold, damp and grumpy folks get in the way of my good mood. As more worse for the weather campers arrived at the fire I stepped away to make room for them. I walked down to the nearby stream and even though it was a little chilly I thrust my hands into the water and brought some of the bracing wetness up to my face and gave it a good washing. It felt good to face the cold with enthusiasm.

A couple of boys nearby looked at me as if I was nuts. I smiled at them thinking: Why should today be different than any other day?

When I got back to the fire Jonesy and Mr. Williams were preparing to make pancakes for breakfast. It occurred to me that it would be fun to help. When I asked if I could be of any assistance, Mr. Williams immediately barked at me to get out of the way.

I probably should have let it go, but I was too charged up with enthusiasm for the day to be shucked off like that. I responded with a polite but firm, "I'd really like to help."

Mr. Williams looked up at me with lightning bolt eyes and said, "Fruitgarden, get the hell out of here!"

As soon as he said that everyone turned to look at him. He had stepped in it and he knew it. Jonesy had a look of shock on his face. I had never heard an adult at camp cuss. Had I backed down at that very moment maybe the future would have been different, but I didn't. I saw an opening and I took it.

"You don't have to cuss at me Mr. Williams I was just offering to help," I said in a slightly hurt voice. "Besides, you never let us cook. You always do it, as if we weren't capable of doing it ourselves."

I looked around for support from some of the other campers and said, "We could cook the pancakes ourselves, couldn't we?"

At first the boys were unsure of how to respond, but as soon as one boy squeaked out a weak, "yes", more of the boys chimed in with "Yes, we can do it!" and "We want to cook the pancakes!" Soon there was a full mutiny in progress, boys were clamoring up to the fire and demanding that we get to cook the pancakes.

220

Jonesy looked as if he had never seen such a thing in his life. Mr. Williams was heating up and looked ready to explode. I thought his eyes were going to start bugging out of his head. It was Maurice that let the steam out of the kettle that was building up pressure by saying to Jonesy, "Dad, why don't you let some of the boys do the cooking this morning? That might be a nice change for you."

I think it was the warm "I'm your son" way that Maurice spoke that got Jonesy to agree. Once that was done all Mr. Williams could do was back away while staring daggers at me. The next thing I knew twenty boys wanted to help and they were all looking at me.

I looked at Maurice for help, but he just sent me a smile and shrugged his shoulders as if to say, "This was your idea!"

Although I had never done this before I had seen it done a number of times so I jumped in and started handing out jobs. There were actually too many helpers now so I had to come up with jobs that didn't really need to be done. Somehow between small stick gathering, paper plate sorting, water carrying and ingredient searching, everyone who had volunteered had some small job to do. I have to admit I was a little concerned about the mixing and cooking part of the process. I was reminded of the time I tried to cook cupcakes, which had been pretty much a disaster. Cupcakes and pancakes sound enough alike that I couldn't help being concerned, in the back of my mind I hoped that things would go better this time.

Complete disaster almost struck when I accidentally knocked over the batter. Fortunately no one was looking and not too much was spilt. I scooped up some of it that didn't look dirty and added a little more water to the batter to make some more volume.

When it seemed safe Ken came over and pitched in to help and I was glad of his experience. We both settled in to do the batter pouring and pancake flipping, with three pans going we had to stay on top of things.

Cooking over the fire was hot work. I soon had my jacket off and was sweating slightly. Once we had a large pile of pancakes staying warm next to the fire we called the rest of the boys over to start eating. The pancakes seem to be coming out pretty well and the compliments started to pile in. I couldn't help noticing that Mr. Williams scowled a lot, but came back for seconds.

When we were done cooking and eating we took the pans over to the creek. We washed them first in the wet sand and then rinsed them in the cold rushing water. Ken was smiling as we finished the task and I asked him what he was smiling about.

"You sure have a way about you, Harry," Ken said. "I have grown up with this camp and been on I can't even say how many campouts. I have never seen anything like that. And getting Mr. Williams to cuss…well, that's going to be talked about for a long time."

I couldn't help protesting, "Ken, all I did was ask to help!"

"Like I said, Harry," Ken responded with a big grin, "You sure have a way about you."

I wasn't sure exactly what Ken was saying. I knew he wasn't criticizing me, but I didn't think he was necessarily complimenting me either. I did seem to be a magnet for trouble, but I wasn't trying to cause trouble, it just seemed to happen around me. Once again I wondered if I was in some subtle way - that I didn't recognize - causing these things to happen.

After cleaning up breakfast Ken and I went to help Maurice saddle up all the horses. Maurice had already started without us but was good-natured about the fact that he had to do more because of the breakfast rebellion. It took about an hour to get all of the horses rounded up and saddled. Then it took another 45 minutes to get all of the boys and their gear on top and ready to ride.

The sun was well up and the day was warming when we started to form our long line once again. Ken and I took up our place in the back and the excitement of the morning receded in our minds, but not apparently in the mind of Mr. Williams.

I reveled in the beauty of nature as we rode through forest and pasture. Birds, fallen logs, tall green grass, streams that made gurgling sounds, all of these were a feast to my eyes, ears and soul: I felt nurtured by nature's aliveness. To the sounds of forest and glade were added the sounds of the horses as they walked and the boys ahead as they talked. I was the very last in line. Ken had gone ahead to help a boy who's jacket had fallen to the ground. I was calm and at peace with the world.

As I passed through a small clump of trees I noticed a small trail that went off to the left side of the main trail we were following. When I got to the juncture I could just barely hear a noise off to the left down the trail. Since Ken was up ahead but not too far away I decided it wouldn't take me long to go find out what the noise was.

I turned Sparky to the left and she responded immediately. It felt like maybe she was up for an adventure as well. Then it occurred to me that walking in line up a trail all day might not be particularly exciting for a horse.

As we moved up the trail the sound that had caught my attention got louder, it was a voice. As I drew closer I began to realize it wasn't a happy voice.

I dismounted Sparky and tied her to a tree. Then I went silently on foot up the trail. The forest was thick so it was absorbing much of the sound. I could hear that a man was yelling at someone but I couldn't tell what was being said.

A short way further down the trail I came to a small clearing and could see and hear what was happening. Mr. Williams was holding the reins of his horse and yelling at the horse to stand still. He had apparently gotten off the horse and was now trying to get back on but the horse didn't want to stand still so he could get his foot in the stirrup to mount.

I recognized the horse, it was Mountain. Mountain was a big horse and also very spirited. He was a sorrel horse; his reddish/orange colored hair was bright and fiery like his temperament. He also had two white socks on his ankles, one on his front right leg and another on his back left leg. I had ridden him several times. He was strong and didn't hesitate to try and take control if he thought he could. Mountain was definitely considered a horse for better riders, you wouldn't want to put a timid rider on Mountain.

I instantly understood what was happening and the dilemma that Mr. Williams found himself in. Mr. Williams had probably come here to answer the call of nature. In the meantime the line of horses that Mountain considered his herd had moved on without him. Mountain wanted to get back to the herd, while Mr. Williams wanted to get back on Mountain. They had the same goal but they were not trying to achieve that goal in harmony with each other.

Mr. Williams was now jerking on the reins as a punishment to Mountain for not standing still, which caused Mountain to feel threatened and be more agitated. Mr. Williams was also yelling at Mountain to stand still, which did absolutely nothing but make things worse. They were looking at each other like mortal enemies and I began to think that things were going to get worse before they got better.

Chapter 31

I suppose I could have made some noise and come into view like I hadn't seen anything. Then I could have offered to hold Mountain while Mr. Williams got on. Of course that would have humiliated him and then he would have been even more upset at me, so I hesitated. In retrospect I wish I had intervened because it would have kept what happened next from happening.

Mr. Williams seemed to be working himself up into a frenzy. He had started talking to Mountain like he expected the horse to understand every word.

"When I say Whoa, I mean Whoa!" Mr. Williams said punctuating every word with a jerk of the reins.

Mountain did not become docile as Mr. Williams hoped he would. Instead Mountain was becoming more agitated and tried to back away. This made Mr. Williams even angrier. The next thing I knew Mr. Williams had reached down to the ground and picked up a four foot long fallen branch of a tree. He then, to my astonishment and anguish, swung the branch at Mountain's neck.

Holding the reins with his left hand he swung the branch with his right hand and it smashed into the middle of Mountains long neck. The power of the blow was so strong that it broke the branch in half. The affect that this had on Mountain was definitely not what Mr. Williams had planned.

Mountain reared up and neighed for all he was worth. His front hooves were well above Mr. Williams's head as they pawed the air. I could see fear in Mr. Williams's face. Mr. Williams instinctively moved back and dropped the broken end of the branch that he was holding. Mountain came down just a couple of feet from Mr. Williams and then he went up again and repeated his performance with a strength of spirit that was truly inspiring.

I could imagine Mountain rearing up for all of the injustices that horses had experienced at the hands of man. He was regal and a worthy representative of his species. I was thrilled with his reaction to Mr. Williams but I was also a little concerned for Mr. Williams. I knew that he was in way over his head now.

I was once again on the edge of intervening when I heard Mr. William's quavering voice try to calm Mountain down. The angry commanding voice was gone, the tones now were of fear and reconciliation. Mr. Williams knew that he had gone too far and was now trying to make amends. What amazed me was that Mountain took his own indignation in rein and began to calm down himself. I think he could tell that Mr. Williams was sincere in his desire to stop the hostilities.

Then Mr. Williams did the first smart thing that I saw him do, he started walking down the trail and leading Mountain rather than trying to get on. Of course the trail was heading in my direction so I had to run as fast as I could to reach Sparky, jump on, and trot up to the rest of the group before Mr. Williams could see me and realize that I had seen the whole thing.

About ten minutes later Mr. Williams came trotting up behind me on Mountain. He had apparently gotten Mountain calmed down enough to mount. I was actually a little surprised that he would even try to mount. And I wouldn't have blamed Mountain if he bucked Mr. Williams off and made him walk all the way back to camp.

Mr. Williams tried to act smug as he trotted by the rear of the line when we reached a meadow that allowed passing. I gave him no indication that I knew what had happened, but I did determine that I would use that information if it ever became necessary. I didn't really like the idea that he was going to get away with doing such a cowardly thing.

The rest of the day I couldn't get the image of Mr. Williams using that branch to hit Mountain out of my mind. I kept thinking of all the mean things that people do to each other and to animals, it really depressed me. I thought of all the problems that I had at home and at school and I thought about wars and disease and death. Earlier in the day I had been focused on how beautiful the world can be, now all I could think about was how the world could also be a harsh place.

Ken seemed to sense that a dark mood had taken me. He gave me space and didn't intrude on my thoughts. I could tell he was concerned about me, but I was so locked into my negative thoughts that I couldn't spare concern for his feelings. I was in a deep pit of unpleasant thoughts and I wasn't ready to come out.

In the afternoon when the group halted for the day a little early; Ken, Maurice and I helped unsaddle all of the horses and turn them once again out to pasture. As soon as we were done I walked off by myself to find a spot to do some private thinking. I walked upstream from the group campsite and kept going until the sounds of the other boys receded and I knew I wouldn't be disturbed.

Under a tall pine tree I found a bed of pine needles that softened the ground as I sat with my back to the tree. The odor of pine seemed to sink into my skin and nerves like soothing vapors. I watched the water of a small stream flow by and tried to release myself from the dark thoughts that had been with me much of the day.

I took a few deep breaths and began to relax. I found the sound of the stream soothing. Peering through the surface of the water I saw some little fish swimming about. They knew nothing of man and the ways of man, I found this thought comforting for some reason.

As I watched the water flow by I allowed my negative feelings to flow out of me and down the stream, I became empty of thoughts. The quieting of my mind was a relief after hours of inner tumult.

I don't know how long I sat there, time didn't seem important. I was just being, in a timeless space.

My quiet was broken when I heard the cracking of a twig behind me in the forest. I turned around to look and found Ken riding up on Lady with Sparky in tow.

Ken reached out to offer me Sparky's reins and said, "Come on."

I didn't question Ken, I just jumped up on Sparky and followed as Ken headed us away from camp.

We were both riding bareback as we moved silently up the trail. I didn't have any idea what Ken had in mind but I was empty and didn't really care. Sitting on Sparky's back I could feel her every move. She was such a strong and beautiful animal. She had been my loyal friend this summer; she was a willing and enthusiastic participant in our various adventures. I patted her on the neck and felt great appreciation and affection for her.

About twenty minutes later Ken and I came to the top of a rise and found ourselves on top of a long ridge that was about fourty feet wide. The ridge was smooth with grass on top and then sloped down on both sides to leave incredible vistas for eyes to feast on. I felt like we were on top of the world, we could see in all directions. There were mountains and valleys filled with a dark green carpet of trees and spotted with flowing light green meadows. In the distance we could see some white from some still unmelted snow of last winter.

About twenty yards down the ridge Ken turned to me and smiled. Then he asked, "Are you ready?"

I didn't know what he meant, but I knew his smile meant he thought I would like it. Then without another word Ken loosened the reins on Lady and leaned forward and whispered in her ear, "Go Lady."

Apparently Lady knew what this meant because she took off like a shot. I didn't even have time to ask Sparky to follow along because she took off before I had fully registered what was happening. Fortunately my body knew what to do before my mind grasped the totality of the situation.

Ken and I had galloped many times on Lady and Sparky, but we had never let them go completely. We had always held them in check to some degree, especially when we rode bareback. This time there was no holding back, the horses were free to run as fast as they dared.

When a rider uses a saddle it is much easier to feel confident about staying on top of the horse. In exchange for confidence and potentially comfort, riding bareback allows the rider to feel more fully the muscles and efforts of the horse, adding a greater sense of speed and oneness with the horse.

As Ken and I raced bareback across that "top of the world" ridge all thoughts of other times and places left me. I was fully present in the moment by moment efforts of Sparky. Her initial leap forward had almost left me behind, but I instinctively leaned forward and held myself low against her neck. Her hooves were like thunder on the ground. She strode forward with amazing speed and agility. She adjusted for the subtle changes in the ground and continued to increase her speed as we seemed to fly like one being across the tall grass that was flowing beneath us like water under a boat.

I could tell that she was fully participating in our quest. I made no attempt to steer her, stop her or make her go faster. She was on her own; I was just along for the ride.

The wind was powerful in my face. Sparky's mane was flowing around my cheeks. I could see Ken and Lady just in front of us, but they weren't ahead by much. Sparky's rhythmic efforts sent my muscles and nerves to new heights of intensity. I found that the more I relaxed, the easier it was to stay balanced on her back. I gave myself fully to the moment and entered into a kind of symbiotic fusion with Sparky.

To say that galloping across that ridge was fantastic, wonderful, stupendous, magnificent, unbelievable, etc., etc. is to downplay how truly thrilling and miraculous it was for me. The horses probably thought they were just finally getting a chance to shake the cobwebs out. Ken had probably run like this many times in his life. For me, it was the culmination of so many converging things that I couldn't fully grasp it.

Just that I could be there in a position to have such an experience was incredible. To have learned to ride well enough in a couple of months to be able to actually do it was also hard to believe. Then to have a friend like Ken who would give me the opportunity to ride such a fantastic horse in this unbelievably beautiful place just added to the...well...it was pretty cool.

I have no idea how far we went. It seemed like an age and a moment at the same time. I think that at some point Ken spoke to Lady again and she started to slow down. Both of the horses were breathing hard but they seemed reluctant to rein in their own enthusiasm. They were fired up with most basic of instincts for a horse: to run.

We let them trot for a while so their muscles would calm down slowly. Then we turned them around and made our way back to camp. Ken and I didn't talk. He could see my face beaming and seemed to understand that talking would diminish rather than enhance the moment.

We had gone quite a way so it took some time to get back. I took in nature's glory as the horses walked side by side. Once again I could say with all my heart that life was beautiful. When we got back to camp and slid off the sweaty sides of our horses I turned to Ken and said, "Thanks."

Ken just smiled and shrugged his shoulders. He knew that the horses and Mother Nature had done the real work, we, had just gone along for the ride.

Chapter 32

That night we didn't build a tent. We spread our ponchos out on the ground and just laid our bags down under the blanket of the sky. When all of the horses were cared for and supper was over I went back to our sleeping bags to get my flashlight. While rummaging around in my stuff I found the box that Shannon had given me.

In the dimming light of approaching night I opened the box. It contained several chocolate chip cookies and a note. As I nibbled on one of the cookies I smiled and read the note:

> Dear Harry Fruitgarden,
>
> Here are some cookies to eat on your trip. I hope you have a good time. I will miss seeing you. Summer is almost over and I am already starting to miss the time we spend together.
>
> Love, Shannon

My smile went from pleasant anticipation to outright ear-to-ear grin. The part of the note that mentioned missing me and love were particularly grin increasing, I read those parts several times.

When Ken showed up and saw me grinning he asked me what was up. I just handed him a cookie and put the note in my pocket. This was private with a capital, very nice.

That night after the campfire I lay for a long time remembering our ride that afternoon. Then I thought about Shannon and her mention of the end of summer made me realize that my adventures at the Circle H Ranch were almost over. Just a few more days and I would be on my way back to the city.

I looked up into the stars and felt the earth beneath me. I was on planet Earth which was tucked away in a solar system on the edge of the galaxy. What is going on out there? Is there life out there in the Universe? And what is the purpose of my life? Why am I here? What is it all for?

At times like this life just seemed so big that I felt too small to face it. What could I, Harry Fruitgarden, do of any consequence for the universe? Then I thought about all of the horses and good people like Ken and his family. That made me think that maybe life could be beautiful even though we don't know a lot about what is going on.

The next day was uneventful if you can use those words to describe a trip that goes through one of the most beautiful places on earth. What I mean is that no one got hurt and nothing dramatic happened to me. I just enjoyed the activities of the day, which mostly meant riding Sparky.

We took our time breaking camp in the morning and then started on the third leg of our journey that would take us back to camp on a different trail than we had left camp. I stayed away from Mr. Williams and managed to have nothing but good thoughts all day.

When we arrived back at camp late in the afternoon all of the boys headed straight for the bunkhouse to clean up. Maurice, Ken and I unsaddled all of the horses and then fed them. That being done we put all of the saddlebags in the truck and drove them to the kitchen where food that was still usable was put away.

I kept my eye out for Shannon, but didn't see her. So I went back to the bunkhouse with my sleeping bag and the few items I had taken on the trip. By the time I got there the water was cold, but the showers were empty. I washed away three days of trail dust and felt renewed.

Tomorrow was the last day I would be here at camp. The day after that would be the first day of the long bus ride back home. The strange thing was that this felt more like home than home. I didn't want to leave, even though I knew there was no choice.

When the supper bell rang I realized that I was hungry. I went along with the crowd and got in line for supper. Once again I looked for Shannon but didn't see her. I saw Mrs. Hutchins and she asked me how the trip had been. I told her it was great. When I saw Mr. Hutchins I told him the same thing. As I talked to them I wanted to say how much I appreciated that they had welcomed me more as a family member than as a camper, but I couldn't find the words.

The evening program that night was lively and entertaining, but I wasn't fully there. My mind had turned towards tomorrow being my last day at camp. I was trying to decide how to spend that last day.

I headed for the bridge after the evening program; I thought I would just stay outside by myself for awhile before going to bed. I stood leaning over the railing looking into the water that was shimmering in the moonlight. I could hear the motion of the water and the sounds of nighttime in the mountains.

My wandering thoughts were lost when I heard the sound of footsteps on the bridge. I looked to see who it was and found Shannon bounding up to me. I had no idea how she found me there, she was like a fairy with secret powers that couldn't be fathomed by mortals. I could just barely see the smile on her face in the dim light.

Shannon didn't waste time with hellos. She grabbed my hand in hers and said, "Meet me by the pig pen one hour after dinner tomorrow." Then she squeezed my hand and bounded off into the night as if she had the night vision of an owl.

I was thrilled that she had found me, though disappointed that she left so quickly. One hour after dinner seemed a long time away. At first I panicked thinking that dinner was supper. But then I remembered that dinner was lunch. Once the momentary panic left me I wondered what she had planned.

Early in the morning of my last day at camp I met Ken, Maurice and Andy at the gate to help feed the horses. When we were done Ken asked me what my plans were for the day. I was amazed at his unassuming style, he didn't want to intrude on my last day unless he was invited. I told him that I was hoping we could take Lady and Sparky out for the morning. He said that would be fine, but he had something he wanted to show me before we went on our ride.

After breakfast we went out to the small corral that was hidden in the trees. There we found a beautiful three year old thoroughbred horse. She was incredibly beautiful. Her almost black coat shimmered in the sunlight and with eyes that danced with youthful zeal she neighed as we approached.

Ken explained that the horse had arrived while we were gone on our overnight trail ride. A horse trader that he knew had left her there knowing that Ken would want her. I was amazed at the trust and relationship that Ken had with this person. Even though Ken had ridden her for only a few minutes yesterday after we got back to camp he definitely knew that he wanted the horse.

Ken asked, "Would you like to ride her?"

Once again I was amazed at the gift of Ken's sharing. He had hardly been on this horse and he was already willing and even eager to share the horse with me. I was touched.

"Yes," I answered with enthusiasm. "I would love to."

I really didn't know what I was saying yes too. I mean, she was a beautiful horse and I knew she was a thoroughbred, but I didn't really know what that meant. There was a part of me that wanted to ride Sparky for old time's sake, but I knew that Ken had something in mind, so I went along with his plans.

We put the saddle that I usually used on the new horse and Ken saddled Lady. Then we rode out towards the capture the flag meadow. Along the way I tried to tune into the new horse. I wanted to get a feel for her personality and to reach out with my thoughts to say, "Hello and welcome."

She had a fast walk and seemed lively. I had the impression she hadn't been ridden a lot because although she seemed willing, she was a little slow to respond to the instructions I sent via the reins. It all made sense, she was young and not much ridden, but she seemed to have a pleasant temperament.

A ways before we got to the meadow Ken started to trot Lady and immediately my horse started to leap forward. I had to rein her back to keep her from running. The horses were nicely warmed up by the time we got to the pasture. I still didn't know what Ken had in mind.

When we got to the entrance of the pasture Ken yelled over to me, "Grab the saddle horn with your right hand!"

I didn't know why he would want me to do that but fortunately I did do it. As soon as Ken had seen that I grabbed the saddle horn he leaned forward and told Lady to run. Once again I was caught by surprise. If I hadn't been holding on to the saddle horn I definitely would have fallen off. This new horse took off like a rocket. I had been impressed with Sparky, but Sparky was an old clunker next to this horse when it came to speed. Even though Ken had intentionally gotten a head start because he anticipated the speed of this new horse, it didn't take long for me to catch and pass Lady almost as if she was standing still. It was unbelievable!

It was like this horse had another gear that Sparky and Lady just didn't have. I couldn't believe how fast I was going. I could hear Ken's shouts of excitement receding behind me as I raced across the pasture leaving him and Lady in the dust. I leaned forward and encouraged my new fleet friend to let loose her youth. We flew across the pasture. The speed and pounding strength of her stride was vibrating up into my whole body. The wind blew my hat right off my head and my red hair started to mingle with the mane of my steed as I held my head close to her neck and we thundered across the field.

I finally had to rein her back as I could see the end of the pasture nearing at an alarming rate. She didn't want to stop but she did start to slow. Fortunately the pasture was wide and I got her to turn slowly to the left while she reluctantly slowed down to what to most horses would consider a fairly hearty run. Then as I made my way back to Ken I got her to slow further and finally break into a trot. She was so full of herself she pranced, raising her front legs high. She seemed to boil over with the fiery blood of her heritage. I knew that I was on an exceptional creature, I felt honored.

238

When we met up with Ken and Lady, Ken was grinning from ear to ear, as was I. He knew he had a winner horse and I knew that I had just had the ride of my life. As we cooled the horses down and retrieved my hat we bubbled with praise for the speed of the new horse. Then Ken turned to me and asked me a question.

"What is her name?" Ken asked.

"I don't know," I answered. "You tell me?"

"No," Ken responded. "You name her."

It took me a second to realize that Ken was asking me to name the new horse. "You're kidding," I said looking right at him.

"No, I'm not," Ken said back with a big grin.

I took seriously the responsibility of naming the new horse. A horse like this deserved a good name. I really wanted to go with something smooth, sleek and elegant. But I knew that there was only one word to express what it felt like to ride her….Rocket. No matter how interesting her personality might be, her speed would always overshadow other qualities.

Unsure if Ken would agree with my choice I mumbled out, "Rocket."

"Rocket," Ken said out loud to get a feel for the word. "Yes, that sure is what she looked like when she went by Lady."

So that was it, Rocket was her name. And I had been given the pleasure and honor of riding her and naming her. I once again felt touched by Ken's gift.

We rode walking side by side for the rest of the morning. We talked about the summer and our lives at home. Ken had become a good friend and I was really going to miss his company. When we got back to the corral and unsaddled the horses I went out and said goodbye to Sparky. She had also been a good friend, I would miss her as well.

Ken and I ate dinner together and then as we were leaving he asked if I had plans for the afternoon. I said yes and smiled. He didn't ask what my plans were, I think he may have guessed, but he didn't say anything, he just nodded with a smile and turned on his way. He was a real gentleman. I admired that.

I went to the bunkhouse and cleaned up after eating. That isn't something I would normally do in the middle of the day, but I felt like it should be done today. I found that for once I wished I had a clock. Exactly what time was one hour after dinner? How would I know exactly when that time had arrived?

Chapter 33

When I reached the pigpen I was all wound up with anticipation. It reminded me of how I felt when I first met Shannon. I thought I had gotten past all that fluttery stuff, but apparently I was wrong. When she finally arrived I was wound as tight as an alarm clock. Fortunately Shannon knew what she wanted to do and how she wanted to act. So I just went along with her until I got myself sorted out.

Shannon grabbed me by the hand and we walked off in a direction that would take us away from camp. We walked in silence for awhile. I just enjoyed holding her hand and being near her. Finally, when we were a fair distance from camp Shannon asked, "How was the camping trip?"

"It was good," I answered.

There was a moment of silence after that and then I said, "I really enjoyed the cookies."

Then there was another pause.

Then I pulled myself together and said, "And I really enjoyed your note...especially the love Shannon part."

Shannon turned and looked me in the eyes. I looked at her. There was something about Shannon that just engaged my heart. I didn't know how or why, she just had that affect on me. I let go of her hand and reached around her and hugged her. We hugged for a long time. We didn't say anything. We just hugged.

That hug was life itself. I can't explain exactly what I mean by that. I just know that I felt something flowing through me that is at the heart of life itself. I wished I could ask Resting Eagle to explain it. I'm sure he would say something wise. All I knew was that my heart was full and life was good.

After our hug Shannon and I talked without stopping for the next two hours. She told me about what she had been doing while I was gone and I told her about the horseback trip. I also told her what I had seen Mr. Williams do with Mountain.

She was shocked when she heard about Mr. Williams hitting Mountain with a branch, but she didn't doubt that I was telling the truth. She asked if I was going to say anything to anyone about it. I told her that I was not unless there was a strong reason. She nodded her understanding without trying to tell me what I should or shouldn't do.

Where did these kind people learn to live this way? I couldn't help asking myself. I was so used to everyone trying to tell me what I should do and how I should think, it was astounding to me to find a whole group of people who didn't act that way.

As the afternoon lengthened I wanted to say or do something that would express my appreciation to Shannon for her friendship. I had thought long and hard about what I could give her, I didn't have much to offer. I had brought little other than clothes with me from home.

When it seemed like I could wait no longer for fear of her saying that she had to get back I spoke up.

"Shannon," I said softly. "I have something to give you."

She turned and looked at me with some surprise.

"But first I want to tell you why I am giving it to you," I continued. I had her full attention. I paused for a moment to gather my thoughts and then plunged in. "I just want to tell you how much I have enjoyed our time together this summer. I have never had a friend like you. I don't mean just that you are a girl. Although it is true that I have never had a girl who is my friend before, I mean that you are a person that I feel I can tell anything to. I have never had a friend like that. It means a lot to me."

Then I ceremoniously took my hat off and put it on Shannon's head. I think she knew how much that hat meant to me. Even still, I was surprised when a tear came to her eye. Then to my even greater surprise she kissed me on the lips.

I was instantly overwhelmed with her presence, both physically and in my heart. It wasn't like you see in many movies where people roll around almost like they are wrestling. It was light and soft. It was calm but deeply felt. I can't say how long the kiss lasted, I just know that it was sweet beyond compare. Then we embraced and just held each other close. I felt enveloped by a person's caring like never before, it touched me to the depths of my being.

We didn't talk much after that. We just sat close together, shoulder to shoulder and appreciated each other's company.

At one point Shannon turned to me and said, "Thank you for being my friend, Harry Fruitgarden." I looked at her and smiled. There was nothing more to say.

It was the supper bell ringing in the distance that forced us to end our time together. We reluctantly walked back to the lodge. When we got close enough to the lodge that others might see us we disengaged our hands. That was hard to do. It was like the true moment of good-bye.

I ate supper that night alone. I was quiet and full of thoughts about life, camp, horses, Ken and the Hutchins family, and of course Shannon.

When it came time for the farewell evening program I sat in the back and kept a low profile. There was singing and skits as usual. Then there was a farewell performance by Shannon and her sisters. Once again I enjoyed not only their singing...but my special friendship with Shannon. Toward the end of their presentation her eyes found me in the back of the room and she gave me a special smile. I really appreciated that.

As the evening wound down I was thinking I would sneak out the side door and make a quiet exit into the night. I was about to make my move when Mr. and Mrs. Hutchins stepped up in front of the group and began to speak.

Mr. Hutchins said, "It has been our pleasure to have you all with us this summer. Those of you who have only been here for a short time have already become good friends and we thank you for that. Others have been here for longer and have become like family. There is one person here who we would like to come forward and receive a new award that we have created in his honor. The Loyal Order of the Chicken, Chicken of the Year Award!"

That announcement made everyone but me laugh. Immediately my "Watch out you are about to be embarrassed!" antennae started to twinge with extra vigor. The next thing I knew Mr. Hutchins was calling out, "Will Harry Fruitgarden please step forward!"

I was now regretting that I had sat in the back. My long journey forward gave all of the boys more time to heckle me with clucking sounds and jeers of "There is the big chicken" and "Give us a big cluck, Harry".

When I arrived at the front of the room I was placed between Mr. and Mrs. Hutchins. They stood guard over me in such a way as to make it clear I wasn't going to escape.

Mr. Hutchins continued with a little speech. "It has come to our attention that Harry has lost his hat."

At these words everyone took notice of the fact that I wasn't wearing my trademark hat. Most of the people here had never seen me without it. Pockets of speculation started to swirl around the room. Everyone wondered what had happened to the hat?

"So, in recognition of his unique contribution to our life here at the Circle H Ranch we would like to make a presentation." Mr. Hutchins proclaimed.

As if it had been practiced to perfection, just at that moment Shannon came out of the dinning hall with my hat on her head and a box in her hands.

It was instantly apparent where my hat had gone. The crowd went wild with hoots and howls. The quieter comments that I probably wasn't supposed to hear ranged from "I can't believe it" to "All right Harry!"

As Shannon stepped up front I was pushed from behind by Mrs. Hutchins to receive my gift.

Mr. Hutchins continued by saying, "So without further ado, we present to Harry Fruitgarden, in appreciation of his help with the horses, his occasional heroics, his unique ability to find trouble, and most importantly, his friendship, we offer this gift as a symbol of our appreciation for his presence here at camp."

Shannon then stepped towards me and handed me the box. She had a big smile on her face and I had trouble focusing on the box and not on her. Mr. Hutchins then gave me a little encouragement by administering a friendly poke to my shoulder. That got me moving and I opened the box.

With the box open I looked inside and became speechless. Seeing my face Shannon could see I needed help, so she reached inside the box and pulled out a beautiful new cowboy hat. After presenting it to the crowd for appropriate applause she placed it on my head.

The rush of emotions that ran through me were coursing through my veins somewhere around the speed that I felt when I was riding on top of Rocket. But the final stroke that made me cry was when Shannon bent forward and kissed me on the cheek in front of everyone including her parents. That was big.

While the boys went wild with the kiss, I was saved by Mrs. Hutchins. Fortunately she chose that moment to get into the act and grabbed me for a big hug. Her embrace gave me time to pull myself together. My life here had been so fulfilling, I couldn't imagine leaving. Yet tomorrow morning I would be on the bus heading back to California. It was hard to believe.

When the evening program was finally over I took the time to say good-bye to all of the people who had made my stay at the Circle H Ranch so meaningful. I was surprised that there were so many. I wasn't used to having a lot of people who cared about me and who I cared about. It made me feel good.

After the last goodnights had been said I went outside and once again stood on the bridge in front of the Lodge. My mind was past thinking about any individual moment of the evening or of the summer. I had achieved some kind of fullness in which I was just that....full: full of good feelings and appreciation.

There was a part of me that didn't want to accept that it was time to leave. At the same time, there was a part of me that knew you can't keep the seasons from changing. The seasons were changing in my life. Tomorrow I would once again be riding in the bus that had brought me here. Soon after that I would have to go back to school. Life around me would go on the same as it had before I came to camp.

The thing that I realized in that moment was that I would be different. I would be fuller with love and appreciation for the good in life. I now realized more about how I could choose what kind of person I wanted to be. The Hutchins family gave me some examples of the different ways that people can be good, not everyone the same, but still good in their own way. I would have to explore myself more to understand how I could become a better person. Maybe this is part of my pact with God to try and be good?

I decided that no matter how things went in my future I would always remember the good that I had experienced here at the Circle H Ranch. I was just turning to head back to the bunkhouse when I heard the patter of feet on the bridge. I looked over to find, once again, Shannon had magically found me in the darkness of night.

She approached me slowly and we embraced without a word. She was wearing my old hat and my new hat got in the way of our hug. We laughed. And then we cried.

In the morning I felt strange not going out to help feed the horses. I probably could have made the time, but somehow I couldn't face it. I had said my goodbye to Sparky and the other horses that were special to me. I would see the other wranglers at the bus when it was time to leave.

By nine o'clock the bus was full and most of the boys were in their seats ready for the long drive. Many of the boys hadn't come this way as a group, they had no idea what the trip would be like. I on the other hand, was not looking forward to it.

My place on the baggage was staked out and I made one last trip off the bus to say my very final goodbye. Everyone was there, Mr. and Mrs. Hutchins, Jonesy and his wife, Maurice, Andy and Ken. The only one that was missing was Shannon.

I shook hands with all of the men, hugged the older ladies, and generally shuffled my feet around hoping that Shannon would show up, while at the same time being afraid I would start to cry again.

I took time to say a special goodbye to Ken. I thanked him for all he had taught me and for sharing his horses and his friendship with me. He gave me his usual shrug and a smile. Then he surprised me by saying, "See you next year!"

It had never occurred to me that next summer even existed. I was shocked that I hadn't thought of it myself. I said with a big grin, "Sounds good to me!"

Just as the bus engine started and I had shuffled my feet as long as I possibly could, Shannon arrived. She came over wearing my hat, which looked pretty darn good on her even though it was a bit big. She handed me a little box and with a big smile and a twinkle in her eyes said, "Thanks for coming to visit us at the Circle H Ranch, I hope you will come again next year!"

Then Shannon stuck her hand out for me to shake. That surprised me a little but I reached out to shake her hand. Once our hands met she squeezed tight and pulled me forward. The next thing I knew she was kissing me again on the cheek. Hoots started up on the bus and then as could be expected, Mr. Williams called out, "Let's go Fruitgarden, this isn't your personal limousine!"

Shannon and I looked at each other for a moment and then I turned back to the bus. Climbing up the stairs past Mr. Williams I experienced one of those "been here before" moments that are called Deja vu. It reminded me of the bus that we took in scouts to Crescent Lake. It also reminded me of the beginning of my trip here to camp, which seemed so long ago.

No sooner had I arrived on my perch in the back of the bus than it started to move forward. I looked out the back window and waved to my Colorado family and especially to Shannon. I would miss this place and these people.

Once the bus was on the blacktop of the main road I took a look at the little box Shannon had given me. When I opened it there was just a piece of paper in it. Unfolding the paper I found a little note.

The beginning of the note started: Dear Harry Fruitgarden. I liked it already. At the end of the note there was a: Please write soon. Love, Shannon. This I liked even more.

In the middle of the note there was no long discourse. It was a simple statement of Shannon's hope for the future. She had written her mailing address.

Here was another way that my new friends were reaching out to say they cared about me and they hoped the future would hold more opportunities for sharing. Why hadn't I thought of asking Shannon for her address? I really could be thick at times.

As the bus wound its way down the road I was flooded with the endless impressions, experiences and inspirations that the summer had brought. Most of all I was thankful for the friendships with both young and old that had filled my heart with a sense of belonging.

Summer camp had held more for me than I ever could have hoped for. Who would have guessed?

For more books by
Lawrence Vijay Girard
go to
FruitgardenPublishing.Com

The
Adventures
of
Harry Fruitgarden
Series

Book #1
What's it All About?

Book #2
Who Would Have Guessed?

Book #3
Someone Should Have Told Me!

Printed in the United States
22562LVS00001B/52-99